D1134748

Chinese Fairytales

Chinese Fairytales

SUN XUEGANG and CAI GUOYUN

Edited by
MEI LAN FRAME

Illustrated by
LEUYEN PHAM

VIKING
an imprint of
PENGUIN BOOKS

Published by the Penguin Group
Penguin Group (Australia)
250 Camberwell Road, Camberwell, Victoria 3124, Australia
(a division of Pearson Australia Group Pty Ltd)
Penguin Group (USA) Inc.
375 Hudson Street, New York, New York 10014, USA
Penguin Group (Canada)
90 Eglinton Avenue East, Suite 700, Toronto, Canada ON M4P 2Y3
(a division of Pearson Penguin Canada Inc.)
Penguin Books Ltd
80 Strand, London WC2R 0RL England
Penguin Ireland
25 St Stephen's Green, Dublin 2, Ireland
(a division of Penguin Books Ltd)
Penguin Books India Pvt Ltd
11 Community Centre, Panchsheel Park, New Delhi – 110 017, India
Penguin Group (NZ)
67 Apollo Drive, Rosedale, North Shore 0632, New Zealand
(a division of Pearson New Zealand Ltd)
Penguin Books (South Africa) (Pty) Ltd
24 Sturdee Avenue, Rosebank, Johannesburg 2196, South Africa

Penguin Books Ltd, Registered Offices: 80 Strand, London, WC2R 0RL, England

First published in China as *zhongguo shenhua* by China Children Publishing House, 2005
This English edition published by Penguin Group (Australia), 2008

1 3 5 7 9 10 8 6 4 2

Design by Cathy Larsen © Penguin Group (Australia)
Illustrations by LeUyen Pham
Decorative elements are traditional Chinese designs courtesy of Dover Books
Typeset in 11/20pt Sabon by Post Pre-Press Group, Brisbane, Queensland
Printed in Australia by McPherson's Printing Group, Maryborough, Victoria

National Library of Australia
Cataloguing-in-Publication data:
Sun, Xuegang
Chinese fairytales / Sun Xuegang, Cai Guoyun; illustrator, LeUyen Pham.

ISBN: 978 0 670 07260 6.

398.20951

puffin.com.au

 This book was published with the support of a grant from SCIO China Book International.

Zhongguo Shenhua

SUN XUEGANG and CAI GUOYUN

Contents

Introduction

This collection of fairytales comes from one of the largest countries in the world, China. As a matter of fact, China is so large that her name in Chinese (中国) means 'Middle Kingdom', for the people of China once believed their country was the centre of the world. In this book you will find fairytales and stories taken from all across this great land, spanning an equally great length of time. For just as China is a large country, it is also a very old civilisation. Two stories in particular,

'Cowherd and Weaving Girl' and the 'The Legend of Lady White Snake', are well over 1500 years old. Yet they are still well-known stories today. 'Cowherd and Weaving Girl' is remembered every Chinese Valentine's Day, and many tourists still visit West Lake Pagoda in Zhenjiang and read about Lady White Snake. In this collection of fairytales you'll find only one version of these wonderful stories, but keep in mind that many versions of each story exist. After all, they have been retold, rewritten and revised through countless generations, so things are bound to change a little.

Although the origins of many of the tales may be a mystery, their themes are quite familiar. Here you will read about dragons, princesses, kings, wizards, wishes and magic . . . universal characters that can also be found in other fairytales and folklore. However, read or listen closely and you will notice important differences. Be on the lookout for dragons who instead of breathing fire, control water and live in oceans and seas ('The Magic Gourd'). Animals are often supernatural beings in disguise ('The Deer Fairy'), while humans can sometimes be animal-spirits in disguise ('The Red Pearls').

Twelve of the eighteen stories in this collection are taken from the fifty-six different people or tribes known as *min zhu ren* (民主人) or the 'ethnic minorities' of China. Each ethnic tale belongs to a group of people who have a unique history, culture, language and, of course, tradition of folklore. Notice the fierceness and bravery of the Mongolian warrior Gunagan, the wit and wisdom of the Tibetan hero Agudengba, and the courage and independence of the Yi heroine Ashima.

Finally, one more point about these tales. Many contain elements of Taoism, a 2500-year-old religion and philosophy of China. 'The Taoist at Lao Shan' is the most obvious example, and it is a humorous tale that warns against learning ancient secrets for one's own glory. Most of the gods and goddesses you'll find in these stories are major deities in Taoism, and whenever you run across an immortal with magical powers you can be sure that he or she is a Taoist.

I hope that in reading this collection of fairytales you will enjoy a magical journey across the varied lands of China and the riches they contain. Look out for the companion volume to this collection, *Chinese Myths*. Together they provide a fascinating portrait of China and its history.

My thanks to all who helped me in working on this project, especially those at Penguin Australia and Penguin China, and my mother, for her help with translations. I would also like to thank Rishi Valley School in India, for providing me with the perfect fairytale cottage at the edge of a beautiful forest to write in.

Mei Lan Frame

Cowherd and Weaving Girl

At the end of Summer, when the nights begin to cool with the approach of Autumn, look up at the night sky and you will see two bright stars sitting across from each another, one on either side of the Milky Way. The names of these two stars are Cowherd Star and Weaving Girl Star. There is an ancient story known throughout China about how these two stars came to be. This story is so well known that it is celebrated every year, but we'll talk about that later, once you know one of the world's oldest love stories.

A long time ago, in fact, a very, very long time ago, heaven and earth were not separated. In those days, the Milky Way touched the earth and lay like a wide, sparkling river across the horizon. The Milky Way was a passage between heaven and earth, and gods and goddesses came down to the human world and ordinary people went up to heaven by crossing this celestial gateway.

On earth, in a poor and remote village, there lived a cowherd boy, who herded cattle from early in the morning until late at night. His parents had died when he was still a child, so he lived with his older brother and sister-in-law. The cowherd's older brother was kind and generous, but his wife was wicked and mean, and treated the cowherd very badly. The cowherd was often hungry and cold, for his sister-in-law would complain that they did not have enough to feed him. She made him live in a shabby cowshed outside the farmhouse. But the cowherd didn't mind; he preferred to stay with the cattle, as they were his faithful companions.

Now, the sister-in-law was constantly thinking of ways

to save money and get rid of the cowherd. One day, as the cowherd entered the farmhouse courtyard, he heard his sister-in-law scolding his brother. 'How worthless you are!' she cried. 'You let your brother eat our food and stay with us when we don't even have enough to feed ourselves. How long do you plan to take care of him? If you won't make a decision to drive him out, then I will!'

The cowherd was very sad when he heard this. Holding back tears, he entered the house and said, 'Brother and Sister, please don't quarrel over me any more. I will leave.'

His sister-in-law quickly replied, 'We have nothing to give you, so don't expect us to help you if you leave.'

But the cowherd only shook his head and said, 'I don't wish for any money from you. All I want is the cattle that I herd every day. They are old and a burden for you to look after anyway.'

The cowherd's brother agreed, and the cowherd silently walked out of the house and rounded up the cattle that had accompanied him for years. Then, bidding goodbye to his brother, he left home.

The cowherd journeyed until he found a suitable piece of land to tend his cattle and build a house. He built a small hut and tilled the land to plant seeds. Although the cowherd was busy feeding his cattle and cultivating his crops, he often felt lonely, for there was no one for him to talk to. At those times, he would lead the cattle to the horizon and sit at the banks of the Milky Way and stare at the stars in the magical sky-river.

One night, when he had led the cattle to the Milky Way, he heard a voice cry out, 'Cowherd! Cowherd!' He looked around, surprised that someone was calling him, but saw no one.

'Cowherd!' he heard again. Looking at his cattle, he saw one of the oxen looking back at him. The ox was speaking to him! Astonished, the cowherd stood up and approached the ox.

'I used to be the Golden Cattle Star in heaven,' the ox said, 'but I did not lead an upright life and was sent back to the human world by the Grand Empress. Because you are honest and kind-hearted, I wish to help you find a companion so you will no longer be lonely. If you come to the riverbank tomorrow at this time, you will see seven fairy sisters bathing in the Milky Way. The most beautiful of the sisters is called Weaving Girl. While she is bathing, you must steal her clothes and hide them. That way, she will not be able to go back to heaven, and must stay on earth and marry you.'

The cowherd listened to the advice of the ox. The next day, he hid himself in the reeds of the riverbank. Soon the fairies came to bathe in the river. While they were splashing in the water, the cowherd swam to the heavenly side of the river and took away Weaving Girl's clothes. Then he swam back to earth and waited.

When the sisters had finished bathing, they got dressed and returned to heaven. But because Weaving Girl couldn't find her clothes, she had to stay in the water.

Cowherd called to her from the riverbank, 'Are you Weaving Girl?'

'Yes, I am,' she answered. 'I've lost my clothes so I can't return to heaven. Who are you?'

'I'm Cowherd, and I have your clothes. I want you to marry me!'

Without her clothes, Weaving Girl could neither step out of the river, nor return to heaven. She had to accept the cowherd's proposal.

Cowherd and Weaving Girl got married. They fell deeply in love with one another and lived a happy, peaceful life together in Cowherd's small hut. After a year, they had twins, a son and a daughter.

Now, one day in heaven is equal to one year in the human world. And Weaving Girl was the granddaughter of the Supreme God and the Grand Empress. So when they realised Weaving Girl had been missing for more than a day, her grandparents began to wonder where she was. They searched everywhere in their heavenly palace but could not find her. Finally, they sent a royal scout to look for her on the banks of the Milky Way. The scout returned with a message that Weaving Girl was living in the human world with a husband and two children. The Supreme God and the Grand Empress were furious!

They gathered their warriors to catch Weaving Girl and return her to heaven. Led by the Grand Empress herself, the warriors crossed the Milky Way and descended to earth.

That night when Cowherd came home, he saw the door to his hut smashed open and his two children sitting on the ground, crying. His son and daughter rushed to him and cried, 'Father, Mother was captured by the Grand Empress. Her warriors have taken her back up to heaven.'

Cowherd ran outside, where his old friend the ox informed him, 'Your marriage must have been discovered by the Supreme God and the Grand Empress. They've arrested Weaving Girl for marrying you. You must go and get her back.'

Cowherd rushed to the banks of the Milky Way, but the Grand Empress had moved the river, and it was now high up in the sky. It shone as brilliantly as before, but it now divided heaven and earth.

He returned home, despondent because he didn't know

how to reach the Milky Way. But the old ox approached him and said, 'Cowherd, I am now old and it is my time to die. After my death, you must remove my hide and make a leather cloak. When you wear this magical cloak, you will be able to fly up to the banks of the Milky Way and find Weaving Girl.'

But Cowherd argued with the ox. 'I don't wish you to die, my friend. I cannot do this.'

'You must do this,' the ox warned him. 'Otherwise, you will never see her again.'

So, upon the ox's death, Cowherd followed his instructions and made himself a leather cloak. Then he grabbed his shoulder pole and fashioned two straw baskets on each end to carry his two children. But his son weighed more than his daughter, so he placed a gourd ladle in her basket to steady the weight of the pole. Finally, he put on the leather cloak and, with his two children, quickly ascended to heaven. When he reached the banks of the Milky Way, he saw Weaving Girl in the distance.

But the Grand Empress, who was leading Weaving

Girl away, also saw Cowherd coming towards them. She took a golden pin from her hair and threw it into the water. All of a sudden, huge waves rose up from the river. They were so high that it was impossible to cross.

Cowherd and his two children saw the waves and cried out in fear. But then his daughter had an idea. 'If we take some of the water from the river,' she said, 'then maybe we can cross it.'

Cowherd took the ladle from his daughter's basket and began scooping out some of the water. His children even used their hands to help him.

Some magpies who were perched on the banks of the Milky Way saw the efforts of Cowherd and his family and were greatly moved. They decided to help them by joining together, one by one, to form a bridge over the turbulent waves of the Milky Way.

When the Supreme God and Grand Empress saw Cowherd and his children approaching Weaving Girl on the magpie bridge, they decided to let them be together, for even nature was in agreement with their love.

But Weaving Girl was a fairy, and therefore not allowed to remain with a human. So, the Supreme God and Grand Empress decided to let them meet on one day of each year, the same day that Cowherd and his family went up to heaven. This day is the seventh day of the seventh month of the lunar calendar. It is the date for the reunion of Cowherd and Weaving Girl on the magpie bridge.

Cowherd and the two children now live in heaven on the west bank of the Milky Way, while Weaving Girl lives on the east bank, alone. They watch each other from across the river. Sometimes they tie letters for each other on the stars that surround them.

If you look up at the Cowherd Star, you will see two little stars on either side. These are his son and daughter. Across from them, on the other side of the Milky Way, is Weaving Girl, and beside her are four stars that form a rectangle. This is the loom that Weaving Girl tirelessly works on while watching her family.

The story of Cowherd and Weaving Girl has been passed down from generation to generation. All people in China refer to the seventh day of the seventh month as China's Valentine's Day. At midday on this day, women go to the temple and place a washbasin filled with water out in the sun and float a needle on its surface. If an image appears in the water, it means they have learned a new weaving technique from Weaving Girl. At night, women also place small tables in their courtyards filled with fruit, needles and string in remembrance of Weaving Girl. They decorate the tables with braided, coloured threads and then string the threads through the needles. Some even put a small spider inside a box and wait until morning to see if the spider has spun a web during the night. A web in the morning ensures good luck for their future work.

And there's just one more thing. When Cowherd crossed the Milky Way on the magpie bridge with his children, his heavy steps trampled some of the feathers on the magpies' heads. That's why you see magpies in China becoming bald at this time of the year, every year.

'Door, Open Tonight!'

A Shui Tale

Once upon a time, in a small town at the edge of Shui Mountain, lived a young girl by the name of Afang. Afang had lovely eyes and a fair complexion, and all the townspeople admired her for her gentle manner and kind ways. But Afang was very poor. She had to work from dawn to dusk as a servant for a rich landlord. She washed clothes, fetched water, cooked food, and never rested from her work until late at night, when she would retire, exhausted, to her small, dreary bedroom.

The landlord was a cruel man. He forced Afang to do more and more work and would only give her scraps of food to eat. He was often in a foul mood and enjoyed tormenting his servants. Sometimes he beat Afang for no reason. Yet Afang's nature was so gentle that she never fought back. She would only go to her room and cry about her misfortune.

One day, Afang was washing clothes at the edge of a river. Thinking about her hardships, a single tear slid down her cheek and dropped into the water. Suddenly, she heard a voice. 'Sister,' said the voice, 'why are you crying? Tell me what has happened to you.'

Afang stood up and looked around the forest. There was no one there. Bewildered and a little afraid, she called out, 'Who's there? Where are you? What do you want?'

Just then, the river began churning and big waves splashed over the banks. In the middle of the river, a pillar of water formed, and out of the pillar jumped a huge, red carp. The carp landed in the water near Afang's feet

14

and announced, 'I am from the palace of the Dragon King and I have been watching you from the river. Tell me, why are you crying?'

At first Afang was too shocked to speak, but seeing that the red carp was friendly and did not want to tease her, she decided to answer him. 'I am busy working day and night at the landlord's house, and I don't have anyone to talk to. My chores are so hard that I find them difficult to bear. That's why I was crying.' Afang paused for a minute and then asked, 'Are you willing to be my friend?'

The red carp flipped its tail back and forth in agreement, sending the river waters churning again. 'Of course, I will be your friend,' the carp replied. 'I'm also lonely, so let's be good friends.'

Afang was delighted to have a new friend. She told the red carp her life story, with all the troubles and burdens she faced. The carp was very sympathetic, and listened with interest until she finished. Then he said, 'Sister Afang, don't be sad. Here, I will give you this ruby.'

The carp swam to the edge of the river and spat out a large, shining ruby from its mouth onto the bank. 'Hit this ruby against any rock on this riverbank and you will see a door appear in the ground. Then say, "Door, open tonight!" three times in a row, and the door will open. You may enter and take whatever treasures you wish. But you must promise to keep this secret and make sure no one else finds out.' Afang promised and watched the carp plunge back into the river and disappear.

That night, Afang couldn't get to sleep. She lay awake in her bed, wondering if what the red carp said was true. Finally, unable to bear her curiosity any longer, she got up and quietly crept out of the still, dark house.

When she reached the riverbank, Afang took the ruby from her pocket and hit it against a rock. Suddenly, right by her feet, a door appeared. She said the words 'Door, open tonight!' three times in a row. The door slowly creaked open, and Afang saw a stairway leading into the ground. Excitedly, she entered the passageway and soon came to a room filled with beautiful clothes and treasures. In the middle of the room was a table set with all kinds of delicious food and wine. A handsome young man was sitting at the head of the table.

'Don't you remember me?' he asked, smiling at her. 'I am the red carp who spoke to you this morning, the son of the Dragon King!'

Afang felt a little nervous, for she had never met anyone royal before. But the young man seemed friendly, and Afang accepted his invitation to eat at the table. After a splendid meal, he took Afang by the hand and showed her the Dragon Palace. Afang felt as if she was in a beautiful dream. Never in her whole life had she had such a wonderful time.

When she was ready to leave, the Dragon Prince gave her a red garment. 'Wear this garment under your clothes,' he told her, 'and you won't feel any pain or tiredness from your work.'

After that night, Afang went often to visit the palace of the Dragon King. With all the good food she was eating, her appearance improved and her body became healthy and strong. And because she wore the magical red garment under her clothes, she no longer felt tired from her work. She wasn't even afraid of the landlord when he beat her, for she had become immune to pain.

The landlord was very angry when he saw that he could no longer torment Afang. He became suspicious and decided to pay close attention to everything she did. One night, he went to her bedroom to check on her. When there was no answer, he broke open the door and saw that the bed was empty. The landlord was furious and ran to Afang's parent's house to find her.

When he arrived, he looked through a window and saw Afang and her family enjoying a grand meal. At the sight of all the food on the table, the landlord was filled with rage. He stormed into the house and overturned the table, then grabbed Afang by her hair. 'Thief!' he shouted. 'You have stolen this food from my house!'

Afang was greatly distressed. She did not want to be called a thief, especially in front of her family, who believed that the food was a gift from a friend. She begged the landlord to listen to her story about the Dragon Palace. But the landlord accused her of lying and threatened to take her to the police. 'Wait!' she cried. 'I have the ruby with me so you can see I'm telling the truth.' She reached into her pocket and placed the ruby in the landlord's hand.

He looked at the shining jewel with greed and said, 'If this is a lie, I'll have you thrown in jail for stealing from me.' Then he took Afang back to his house and locked her in her room.

That night, the landlord went to the riverbank. He took out the ruby and did exactly as Afang instructed. As the door to the Dragon Palace opened, the landlord hesitantly entered the passage. But when he saw the room was filled with treasures, he quickly forgot his fears and dashed around, stuffing jewels and gold into his pockets. The next morning, the landlord was so happy with his new wealth that he even forgot to punish Afang, and spent the whole day gloating over his treasure.

On the second night, the landlord arrived at the

riverbank carrying a number of bags. He took out the ruby and said, 'Door, open tonight!' three times. Just as it had the night before, a door opened in the ground. But the Dragon King had discovered the landlord was stealing his treasures and had decided to punish him. When the landlord stepped through the door, he fell into a giant hole. No one ever heard from him again.

At daybreak the next morning, Afang ran to the river-bank to confess to the red carp that the landlord knew her secret. She shouted for the red carp to come and listen. When the red carp arrived, he quickly told her the fate of the greedy landlord, and assured her she never had to worry about being bullied by him again. As she listened, Afang began to cry.

'But why are you crying?' asked the carp.

'Because I no longer have the ruby,' she said. 'I'll never be able to visit the palace again.'

'Do not worry,' said the carp. 'Come tonight and take an ordinary white stone from the riverbank. Knock it against a rock and you'll be able to visit once more.'

That night, Afang took a white stone from the river and followed the carp's instructions. She entered the palace, but the Dragon Prince was not there. Afang saw an empty glass bottle sitting on the table and placed the white stone from the riverbank inside. Instantly, the bottle filled with silver. Afang left the palace with the silver and returned to her family. They bought farmland and livestock, and together led a rich and peaceful life. Afang no longer had to worry about being poor.

Time passed, and soon Afang had reached the age of marriage. One day, a handsome man carrying many gifts appeared at her door. When Afang saw him, she immediately recognised him as the Dragon Prince and ran to embrace him. They married in a huge celebration attended by all the townsfolk, and together lived happily ever after.

The Invisible Bird

A JINGPO TALE

If you visit Jingpo Mountain in China, you will see that it is home to many exotic, colourful birds. Each morning, when the first rays of the sun spill into the woods, the birds wake up and begin to sing, until the entire mountain is filled with a melodious concert. If you are very lucky, you might see amongst these birds a very precious and beautiful bird, the golden kingfisher. The Jingpo people believe the golden kingfisher is the bird of happiness, and that seeing one brings joy and good luck. Why do they believe this? Well, it all goes back to a very old story . . .

A long time ago, in a pine-forest village called Golden Bamboo Village, there lived a spirited young man and his mother. This young man was known for his kind-heartedness, as he was always willing to help others. The people living in his village were very poor, and many would starve when their harvests yielded too little. Even though this young man was also poor, he was a skilled hunter and always shared whatever he caught. He gave deer, pheasants and rabbits to the other villagers so they had enough to eat during hard times.

One day, the young fellow journeyed into the mountains to collect firewood. After finishing his task, he started down the mountain to return home, when he spotted a golden kingfisher perched on the branch of a tree. The bird looked at the young man and began to sing. It seemed as if the kingfisher was calling to him, so the young man carefully approached the tree and stretched out his hand. But just then the bird disappeared. The song, however, continued. Even though the young man had never heard of anything like this, he knew the golden kingfisher

was still on the branch. He gingerly reached towards the sound with his hand, and soon felt the soft feathers of the bird. Immediately, the golden kingfisher reappeared. The young man gently cupped his hands around the bird and set off home, happy and excited with his catch.

News of the golden kingfisher spread rapidly through the young man's village. The village magistrate heard the story and decided to bring the matter to the court wizard. The magistrate was a small-minded and selfish man, and he often consulted with the wizard to see how he could benefit from any situation. But the wizard said the kingfisher was a bad omen, and he told the magistrate to drive the bird out of the village. 'If you don't,' he warned, 'there will be no peace for you here again.'

As soon as he heard this, the magistrate ordered some of his men to set fire to the young man's house.

The young man and his mother were resting when they heard several men approaching their house. They were afraid, but the kingfisher called them to his cage with his gentle song. When the young man and his mother touched the cage, they became invisible. In this way, they were able to escape from the village with the golden kingfisher. They soon found a spot in the mountains and built a hut, where they lived by hunting and fishing. The young man took the golden kingfisher with him on hunting trips, and he was invisible wherever he went. Because no animal could see him, the young man was always successful in his hunting, and he and his mother lived an easy life together in the forest.

One day, the young man was high up in a tree, picking some fruit. Suddenly, he spotted a large boa slithering across the ground with a gold ring in its mouth. The young man quickly threw a piece of fruit from his basket toward the snake. The boa immediately let go of the gold ring and began to eat the fruit. The young man threw another piece of fruit, then another, getting further away each time, until the boa had slithered away from the tree and into the forest. Then he jumped down and picked up the gold ring.

As he looked at the gold ring in his palm, his body

started to rise up into the air. He put the ring on his finger and flew a great distance, finally arriving at a bamboo house he had never seen before. The young man pushed open the door and entered the house, where he saw an old lady cooking by the fire. She was very happy to see him and kindly invited him to join her for dinner. Though he was hungry, the young man turned the invitation down, explaining that his mother was waiting for him and would not eat until he returned. The woman was touched by the young man's love for his mother, and she took a copper pot hanging on her wall and presented it to him as a gift. 'Take this back with you,' she said. 'When you are hungry, knock on its side three times and it will be filled with whatever food you want.'

The young man accepted the copper pot, thanked the old woman, and flew back to his hut. There, he found his mother waiting for him. He sat down and quickly told her everything that had happened. When he finished, he showed her the copper pot and placed it between them. Both the young man and his mother knocked on its side three times and said, 'Please give us a pot of rice.' As soon as they had finished speaking, the pot was filled with hot, fragrant rice. The mother and son were speechless with surprise and happiness. Never again would they have to worry about food.

Back in the village, the magistrate heard about the wonderful gifts that belonged to the young man and his mother. He realised that the kingfisher actually brought good luck instead of being the bad omen the wizard had led him to believe, and he decided to take the bird by force.

That night, a gang of men arrived at the front door of the hut. But this time, the young man was prepared. He placed the golden kingfisher in his mother's hands and led them to a safe hiding spot in the forest. Then he went back to the house and, in full view of the men, slipped the gold ring on his finger. He rose up in the air and flew here and there. When the gang of men ran to catch him, he led them through the dark forest toward the steep cliffs of the mountain. A few of them crashed into trees and were knocked unconscious. Others fell to their deaths over the edge of the cliffs.

After defeating the magistrate and his men, the young man and his mother returned to the village and told the villagers how the magistrate had tried to kill them. Realising that the magistrate was a selfish and evil man, the villagers drove him out of the village. The young man became the new magistrate, and the villagers enjoyed a richer, happier life.

And what of the golden kingfisher? Well, when the young man realised that the bird could help everyone by bringing them good luck, he released it into the woods in order to give others the chance of a happy life.

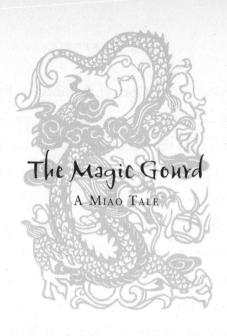

The Magic Gourd

A Miao Tale

Long ago, in a remote mountain village in southern China, there lived a prosperous old man and his three sons. The old man was happy with his three talented, well-respected sons and, knowing that he would soon have to decide who would be the new head of the family, he decided to set them a task. At the beginning of the twelfth lunar month, he summoned them for dinner at his house.

'My three sons,' he announced during dinner, 'today is the first day of the month and, as you all know, I will be eighty years old on the thirtieth day of this month. On that day, I must decide which one of you is to take my place as the head of the family.'

'But father,' the eldest son protested, 'you still have many years before you. It is not necessary for us to discuss this now.'

But the old man would not change his mind. 'My sons, you are all equally capable and talented,' he continued. 'So I have decided to set you all the same task. You are to leave the village and bring back as many gifts for my birthday as you can. Whoever brings back the most gifts will become the head of the family. I will give you each one hundred taels of silver to spend. Remember, it is the number of gifts that will determine which of you will take my place. Now, rest here tonight, for tomorrow morning you must leave on your journeys.'

The three sons agreed and went to sleep, each dreaming of the gifts they would bring to their father.

The next day, when the sun had barely risen above the horizon, the three sons set off from their father's house.

Soon they came to a fork in the road, which split into three paths. The eldest son chose the path on the left, the second son the path on the right, and the youngest son the middle path. Wishing each other safety and luck on their journeys, they promised to meet again at the same fork three days before their father's birthday.

After saying farewell to his two elder brothers, the youngest son set forth on the middle path. Being care-free in nature, he sang as he walked and thought happily about the task he had undertaken. Soon the path opened onto an expanse of green pasture, dotted with herdsmen and cattle. The youngest son heard beautiful music coming from a group of herdsmen, yet he could not recognise the sound of the musical instrument. He approached the musician and asked him the name of the instrument.

'It is called the Wuba,' the musician replied. 'It's the most popular instrument in our lands.'

'Really?' cried the youngest son. 'I've never heard or seen one before! Its music is so beautiful; I must have one and learn how to play it. Can you teach me how to play?'

'Of course,' answered the musician, and without hesitation he invited the youngest son to join the group.

The youngest son spent three days and three nights with the musician and perfected the art of playing the Wuba. By the end of his training, he could play so exquisitely that his music sounded as if it were coming from heaven. The youngest son was very pleased and gave the musician the one hundred taels of silver in payment. Carefully wrapping up his Wuba, he said goodbye and headed southwards.

Soon he reached the coastline of the South China Sea. It was dusk when he arrived, and the afterglow of the setting sun painted the water red and gold. Touched by the beautiful surroundings, he sat down on a rock and began to play his Wuba. The youngest son became entranced in his playing, and soon the night winds came and carried his melodious music out to sea, all the way to the home of the Dragon King.

The Dragon King lived far below the water, in his magical Dragon Palace that shone deep blue and green.

He was celebrating his royal birthday, and all the court officials had gathered for a grand feast in his honour. The music from the Wuba entered the palace softly at first, but soon grew into a distinct melody, intriguing all the officials with its divine sound. When the music reached the ears of the Dragon King, he stopped the feasting and asked where the music was coming from. Since no one knew, the Dragon King immediately sent one of his servants to locate the source of the music.

Meanwhile, the youngest son continued to play his Wuba on the shore. Suddenly, to his amazement, he saw a man dressed in royal colours appear out of the waves and walk towards him! The youngest son continued to play as the strange man approached.

'Sir,' said the royal servant, 'what is this instrument you are playing?'

'It is called the Wuba,' the youngest son replied.

'Well, it is the wish of my lord the Dragon King that you bring your Wuba to our palace beneath the sea and entertain us with your music.'

Although he was astonished by the request, the youngest son quickly agreed and the two of them set off for the Dragon Palace.

The Dragon King was delighted by the youngest son's musical talent and invited him to perform at the banquet. The music so entranced everyone in the royal audience that the youngest son was asked to stay for a few weeks. He happily accepted the invitation and played the Wuba every day for the Dragon King and his court. In addition, he taught the King's sons and grandsons to play. Yet the youngest son could not forget his father's birthday and the promise to meet his two brothers. One day, he asked for permission to go home. In return, he would leave the Wuba as a gift for the royal court.

While preparing to leave, the youngest son was approached by the third prince of the royal family. 'Sir, if my father offers you a reward, do not ask for any of his treasures,' advised the royal prince. 'Instead, you should ask for the plain gourd in his possession.'

Hearing that the youngest son was ready to depart,

the Dragon King summoned him to his throne. 'The time has come to say goodbye,' said the Dragon King. 'However, because of your generous gift of music to my kingdom, I wish to grant you a handsome reward.' The Dragon King stood up and parted the curtains behind his throne, revealing a treasure room filled with gold and jewels. 'What treasures do you want?' asked the Dragon King. 'You can take whatever you like.'

But the youngest son answered that he desired no treasure except the plain gourd in the King's possession. The Dragon King agreed and presented the gourd to the youngest son.

The youngest son arrived back at the shore and began his long journey home. After travelling for a while, he became tired and decided to rest at the side of the road. He was curious about his gift, so he took out the gourd and opened the lid. To his great surprise, out from the gourd jumped a tiny man.

He looked at the youngest son and said, 'Master, what is your wish?'

The youngest son answered, 'I want a horse.'

Immediately, a beautiful red horse appeared in front of him. The youngest son quickly put the lid back on the gourd and jumped onto the magical horse. He travelled rapidly and soon, two days ahead of schedule, he arrived at the fork in the road. He eagerly awaited his brothers' return. Finally, he saw his elder brothers approaching from a distance, both of their packs filled with exotic gifts and treasures.

'What did you bring back for our father?' they asked.

'I don't have anything except this plain gourd,' answered the youngest son.

The elder brothers were very angry when they heard this and scolded their younger brother, telling him he was worthless, especially because he had spent all his money as well. But the youngest son only smiled at their comments and silently followed his brothers on the three-day journey home.

The old man was very pleased when his sons arrived back home. He looked at the many gifts and treasures in their packs and asked expectantly, 'Are all of these my birthday gifts?'

The elder sons answered together, 'These are the gifts selected by us. Younger brother, however, spent all his money and brought nothing back for your birthday.'

When he heard this, the father was furious. 'You are the most useless of all my sons!' he yelled. 'Go to the firewood shack outside and don't let me see you in this house tonight.'

The next morning, on his father's eightieth birthday, the youngest son took the gourd from his pack. Just like before, a tiny man appeared and asked, 'Master, what is your wish?'

'Build a grand palace for me and prepare a delicious banquet in honour of my father,' the youngest son replied. 'Let it be more wonderful than anything the people here have ever seen.'

Suddenly, the firewood shack was transformed into a splendid palace. Inside was a luxurious banquet, far greater than anything the youngest son had ever seen, even when he'd stayed at the Dragon Palace.

The old man and his eldest son came rushing out of the house. They were astonished by what they saw.

'My father,' said the youngest son, 'I give you this feast to honour your eightieth birthday.' The youngest son bowed three times to his father, and then invited all the people in the mountain village to join the feast.

Soon, news reached the emperor that there was a magic gourd capable of granting wishes in the village. Hoping to get his hands on it, the emperor gathered his army together and proceeded to the village. When he reached the palace, he was angered to see that it was bigger and more impressive than his. He confronted the youngest son and said, 'Give me a palace that is more splendid than this, or I will kill all of your family.'

The youngest son was enraged by the emperor's demand, but he was also wise enough to recognise the emperor's true nature. He took out his magic gourd and showed the emperor how to make a wish. In a matter of seconds, an even more handsome palace appeared.

The emperor was greatly impressed. He thought, 'I can get whatever I want with this magic gourd. To have such a thing is even better than being an emperor.' So the hasty emperor said to the youngest son, 'I will exchange my throne for this gourd.' Taking out the imperial seal from his pocket, the emperor cried, 'Look, here is the imperial seal, and now you are the emperor!' Without waiting for the youngest son's consent, the emperor shoved the imperial seal in his hands, grabbed the magic gourd, and quickly left the village.

The emperor could hardly wait to try out the magic gourd. He took off the lid and exclaimed, 'Give me a red pavilion in the sky.' Immediately, a red pavilion appeared in the air. The emperor hurriedly climbed onto it. But after walking the length of the pavilion, he soon grew bored. He took out the magic gourd again and said, 'Make this pavilion disappear.' Yet the pavilion was built in the air, which the emperor forgot in his greed and haste. So when it disappeared, the emperor fell from the sky, and was blown away by the wind.

The youngest son, however, was very content with his end of the bargain. He moved all his family into the imperial palace and lived many years as a good and just emperor.

How the Rats Found Their Son-in-Law

In China, the New Year celebrations last a whole week. On the first two nights, people often stay awake all night long. But on the third night, it is tradition for children to go to bed early. Once the evening meal has finished, mothers will say to their children, 'Time for bed! The rats are getting married tonight, and you must sleep so you won't disturb their marriage ceremony.' But what is the reason behind this tradition? Well, that's an interesting story . . .

Once upon a time there was a family of rats. Rat daughter grew up and soon it was time to find her a husband. Her parents looked at her and thought, 'We are the first of the twelve zodiac animals, so our status is very high. Therefore, we must find the greatest bridegroom in the world, because only such a bridegroom would be a worthy match for our daughter.'

Rat father and mother thought for a long time about who their future son-in-law should be. Finally, they decided to travel far and wide to search for him.

They began their journey by asking those they met the question, 'Who is the greatest in the world?' All the people pointed above their heads and said, 'The sun! The sun is the greatest. He gives light to the world and without him everything on earth would perish.'

Rat father looked up at the sky. It was so bright that he could hardly open his eyes. He and Rat mother decided to climb the East Mountain, where the sun resided. When they finally arrived after the long climb, they saluted the sun and said, 'Sir, we hear you are the greatest in the world. Will you be our son-in-law?'

The sun blushed red and said, 'Mr and Mrs Rat, thank you for your praise. Yet I am not the greatest in the world, because I am afraid of something.'

Rat father was surprised and asked, 'Who are you afraid of?'

'I am afraid of the cloud,' the sun said. 'Although I bathe the earth in sunshine, whenever the cloud comes he can block my rays completely.'

Rat father and mother had to agree. They said good-bye to the sun and began to look for the cloud.

After some time, they found the cloud, resting against a mountainside in a peaceful and silent valley. Walking towards him, Rat father called out, 'Mr Cloud! We hear you are the greatest in the world and that even the sun is afraid of you. Will you be our son-in-law?'

The cloud shimmered after hearing the compliment. He lowered himself to the ground and said, 'Thank you for your praise. Although I would be honoured to marry your daughter, I must tell you that I'm not the greatest.'

'Why?' Rat mother asked. 'We heard from the sun that even he is afraid of you.'

'That is true,' answered the cloud. 'But when the wind comes, I am dispersed into nothing. Also, I must cooperate with the wind to block the sun, so he is greater than I am.'

Then Rat father and mother realised there was no wind in the valley. That was why the cloud had chosen to rest there. Considering the cloud's words, they decided to look for the wind.

But it was difficult to find the wind because he never stayed in one place. Rat father and mother spent a long time and walked a great distance before they found him.

The wind laughed heartily when he heard the Rats' proposition, which made the treetops rustle in delight. He spoke very rapidly, saying, 'I can blow. I can disperse the cloud. I can blow off people's hats. I can cause leaves to swirl and I can even bring down huge trees. Yet I am not the greatest, because I am afraid of the wall.'

Rat father and mother looked at each other in disbelief. 'But you are so powerful!' they said. 'Why are you afraid of the wall? He cannot move like you.'

'It is precisely because the wall does not move that he is greater than me,' said the wind. 'When the wall encircles an area and makes a room, I cannot blow into that room. So, you see, the wall is much greater than I am.'

Rat father and mother were greatly discouraged. They saw the truth of the wind's argument, but everyone they had met had a reason why there was one who was greater. At this rate, their search would never end. However, since they still wanted to find their future son-in-law, they decided not to give up. They said goodbye to the wind and went to look for the wall.

When they found the wall and told him their proposition, they hoped he would agree that he was the greatest. Yet he only stood firm and asked, 'Don't you two know who I'm most afraid of?' Rat father and mother shook their heads, confused. The wall smiled, which made his plaster creak, and said, 'I am afraid of rats the most.'

Rat father and mother looked at each other in shock.

'That's right,' said the wall. 'A cloud cannot bring me down, nor can the wind. Even the sun cannot defeat me when people hide in my shade. But I am not the greatest in the world, for I am powerless to stop you rats from making a hole in me! You rats are the greatest in the world.'

Rat father and mother smiled. 'Yes, we are great, too!' they exclaimed. 'Why, we've been disregarding ourselves the whole time!'

So, after travelling throughout the world searching for the perfect son-in-law, they were surprised to find themselves returning back home. They decided to find their son-in-law among the rats.

They set their daughter's wedding day for the third evening of the first month of the Chinese calendar. Many rats came together and formed a procession to welcome the bride. They played the drums, banged on gongs, set off fireworks, and lifted high the bride's sedan chair.

If you're wondering why rats get married in the first month, it's because the rat is the first of the twelve zodiac animals and therefore should marry in the first month. Rats always marry on the third day of the New Year, because people are tired from the first two days of celebrations and it's nice and quiet!

The Deer Fairy

A LI TALE

On Hainan Island in the South China Sea, there is a famous peninsula called 'Deer Looking Back'. The hills of this peninsula look like a deer whose head is turned back towards the centre of the island. A local legend of the Li people tells us how this place got its name.

A long time ago, at the foot of the magnificent Wuzhi Mountain, there lived a mother and her son. The mother was elderly and often in poor health, but her son, Alang, was only twenty years old. He always took great care of his mother when she was sick and tried to make her life more comfortable. He was also a skilled hunter and provided food for them both.

High above Wuzhi Mountain, in the heavenly world, lived the fairies. The fairies dressed in beautiful clothes and lived a carefree, luxurious life in splendid palaces. But there was one young fairy by the name of Abin who often felt lonely and unhappy. She had heard about the human world and was filled with curiosity about what life was like there. She longed to visit, but the Grand Empress of the fairies was very strict. 'It is the law of the fairies,' said the Grand Empress. 'We do not visit the human world, especially out of idle curiosity. Their world is different from ours. You are not allowed to go.'

Abin became very sad, for she could not think of a possible way to leave heaven. Then one day an opportunity came. The Grand Empress was throwing a Peach Banquet, a huge celebration where all the immortals, gods and goddesses gathered at the Empress's palace for feasting and drinking. Abin knew that everyone would be so caught up with the festivities that they would not notice her absence. In the middle of the celebration, she quietly slipped out of the palace and flew down to the human world.

But the Grand Empress already knew what Abin was planning to do and had decided to test her. When Abin entered the human world, she was transformed into a small, helpless deer.

It was late afternoon by the time Alang had finished hunting in the woods of Wuzhi Mountain. He was heading down the mountain with his catch for the day when suddenly he heard a great crashing through the trees. A little deer appeared running towards him, pursued by a wild boar. The little deer was limping badly, and Alang knew it would soon fall prey to the rapidly approaching boar. He quickly threw the pheasant he had killed into the woods. Diverted by the smell, the boar changed direction and ran after it. Meanwhile, the little deer lay under a tree, trembling with fear. Its right leg had been slashed by the boar and was bleeding profusely. Approaching slowly, Alang took some herbs from his pack and put them on the wound. Then he bound the wound, touched the deer's head gently and left. The deer's eyes shone with softness and gratitude as it watched the receding figure of Alang. The deer was the fairy Abin.

When Abin returned to heaven, she could not forget the hunter Alang. His brave actions, so kind-hearted and caring, took up all her thoughts. She knew that she had fallen in love with him, and was determined to return to Wuzhi Mountain.

A short time after, Alang's mother became very ill. Alang brought her many kinds of medicine, but nothing worked. Within a few days, his mother had grown so weak that he feared for her life. Because he could not go hunting, there was no food in the house. But Alang knew his mother must eat to maintain her strength, so he asked his neighbour to look after her. Shouldering his bow and arrow, Alang left in the morning for the forests of Wuzhi Mountain.

Despite the clear weather on the mountain, Alang could not find a catch the entire day. He was about to head home, when suddenly a beautiful deer appeared directly in his path. The deer looked at Alang and stood perfectly still. Puzzled, Alang slowly approached it. The deer stepped back, matching Alang's footsteps, but did not run away. It just continued looking at him, steadily. Alang reached for his bow and pointed it at the deer. Yet, the deer still wouldn't move. Frustrated, Alang ran towards it, and the deer finally took off. Together, they ran over ninety-nine mountains and crossed ninety-nine rivers until they reached a cliff on the southern side of the Sanya Gulf.

With the edge of the cliff at its back, the deer had nowhere to go. Alang again took out his bow and pointed it at the deer. He was just about to release his arrow, when suddenly the eyes of the deer turned towards him, looking at him with great love. Sensing for the first time that there was something special about the deer, Alang lowered his bow. To his amazement, the deer transformed into the most beautiful girl Alang had ever seen.

The deer girl told Alang that she was Abin, a fairy from heaven. She explained that because she was forbidden to visit the human world, the Grand Empress had turned her into a helpless deer. But Alang had rescued her from the boar, and shown her kindness and compassion. Afterwards, when she had returned to heaven, she could not forget Alang's great deed. She confessed to the Grand Empress that she had fallen in love with a human. The Grand Empress did not believe that true love existed in the human world, so she decided to return Abin to earth in the form of a deer. If Alang demonstrated the same noble feelings again, then she would allow Abin to remain in the human world and marry him.

Alang was very happy to hear Abin's story. He took her hands in his own and said, 'I am pleased and honoured to accept you as my wife. You have brought me great happiness.'

Abin smiled gently and said, 'If you had not pursued me all the way to this place, perhaps my plan would not have worked. I am thankful for your persistence.'

Then she took a seed out of her mouth and planted it in the ground by their feet. As she sang a song the seed was a witness to their love, and a tiny sprout grew up from the ground. Soon a full-grown tree laden with fruit stood above the heads of the two lovers. Abin picked some of the fruit and together they made the long journey back to Wuzhi Mountain and Alang's home.

When they arrived, Alang discovered that his mother was so ill she could barely move or speak. Abin quickly knelt beside the bed and gave Alang's mother the fruit to eat. After eating the fruit, Alang's mother slowly opened her eyes and then sat up. She was overjoyed when she heard that Abin was a fairy who had come to marry her son, and was fully recovered by nightfall.

Abin and Alang lived a happy life together with Alang's mother. They went on to have many children. Their children named the peninsula where their parents met 'Deer Looking Back'. Even today the magical love story about Alang and Abin is famous throughout the region.

Lover Cloud

A BAI TALE

In southern China, the Dali region in the Yunnan province is well known for its spectacular lakes and mountains. The beautiful scenery has also inspired many folk myths and legends. Of these stories, 'Lover Cloud' is probably the most famous.

A long time ago in Dali, there lived a king by the name of Nanzhao. King Nanzhao had a very beautiful daughter, and by the age of nineteen she had already drawn the attention of many noblemen from all over Yunnan.

Hoping to win the young princess's hand, her suitors arrived at the palace bringing gifts and riches. Yet the princess remained unimpressed. Regardless of their wealth and refined appearance, she thought these men boastful and lazy. She wanted her future husband to be a brave and noble man.

One day during the Raoshanling festival in the fourth month of the year, the princess was walking in the forest when she came across a tall and handsome hunter. They started talking and, even though they had just met, they felt as if they had always known one another. The princess learned that the hunter lived alone, high up in a cave on Yuju Peak. He was an orphan and lived a simple life in the forest, hunting for food and keeping little in way of possessions. As the afternoon wore on and the sun's rays began to slant through the trees, they realised they had fallen in love. Before the princess returned to the palace, they swore to be together always.

But when the princess arrived home, she was summoned by her father, the king. He happily announced that he had great news. 'My daughter,' he began, 'today I met a rich general. I have promised you to him. You will marry him soon, on the first auspicious day of this month.'

The princess was greatly distressed by her father's news. She told the king that she had fallen in love with someone else, and begged him to call off the wedding.

Her father was furious. 'How can a princess decide on her own marriage!' he shouted. 'No, you will obey me and marry this general. It has already been arranged.' The king stormed away, and then ordered his soldiers to lock the princess in the palace. Under no circumstances was she allowed to leave.

Inside the palace, the princess was overcome with sadness and refused to eat or drink. She cried all day and night, despairing that she would never see her beloved hunter again.

One morning, the princess was sitting at her window when a small magpie flew up and perched on the sill. 'Please don't cry,' the magpie told the princess.

'I will find the hunter on Yuju Peak and he will come and save you.'

The magpie quickly flew away and told the hunter news of his loved one. Straightaway, the hunter set off for the palace to save the princess.

On his way, he came across an old man sitting on a log. The hunter went to hurry past, but the old man cried after him, 'Boy! I see a fire burning on your forehead. Why are you in such a hurry?'

The hunter stopped and turned to the old man, sighing. 'I must make haste to save my beloved, a princess who is locked in the palace by her father.'

The old man was thoughtful for a moment. 'To save the princess, yes,' he replied, 'but that palace is heavily guarded. How can you, a lone hunter, save the princess?' Rising from his seat, the old man hobbled close. 'I've heard there is a peach tree on the cliffs of Fengyan Cave,' he whispered. 'If you find it and eat its peaches, then you will indeed be able save your princess.' When he finished speaking, he suddenly disappeared.

The hunter realised what had just happened. He had been in the presence of a heavenly being. He bowed three times in the direction where the old man had vanished, and quickly went on to Fengyan Cave.

The cliff face of Fengyan Cave was so steep it looked as if it had been cut with a knife. Its peak was hidden in clouds, while below lay a great abyss. Yet the hunter was so eager to save the princess that these difficulties did not bother him. He scrambled to the top of the cliff and there, in the middle of the fog, was an enormous peach tree. The hunter approached the tree, picked a large red peach from its branches and bit into the fruit. After one bite, he felt a great energy flowing through his body. After finishing the whole peach, he had the power to fly through the sky like a bird.

The hunter flew a vast distance to arrive at the palace. When the princess saw him at her bedroom window, she ran towards him and embraced him. They set off through the moonlit night for Yuju Peak, and were married in the hunter's cave.

The king was furious when he found out his daughter had disappeared. He went straight to the home of an evil wizard called Luoquan and commanded him to get the princess back. Using his magic light, the wizard saw the princess and the hunter together on Yuju Peak. He sent a crow to their cave, with a message that the princess must return home immediately. 'Otherwise,' the crow warned the princess, 'Luoquan will raise an enormous blizzard and you and your hunter will freeze to death.

But the brave princess dismissed the crow's warning by saying that she would stay with her hunter in death as well as life.

When the wizard heard the princess's answer, he removed a magic bottle from the folds of his cloak. Uncorking the bottle, Luoquan began to chant a spell. Suddenly, the sky went black and began to hail. A winter storm approached from the horizon and the temperature dropped to freezing as heavy snow began to fall. Soon the entire mountain of Yuju Peak had turned to ice.

In the cave, the princess was shivering and slowly

losing strength, when the hunter had an idea. 'Don't worry,' he said. 'I too have magic power. I will fly to the wizard's home and bring you his cloak. Then you'll be safe from the cold.'

The princess thought the idea was too dangerous, and begged the hunter not to go. But he assured her that he would return soon and quickly flew away.

Little did the hunter know he had fallen into a trap. When he reached the evil wizard's home, he saw the cloak on a chair and went to pick it up. As soon as he touched it, he felt all his magic strength leave him. Seeing that the hunter was now weak, the wizard grabbed him. But the hunter struggled out of the wizard's grip and fled outside.

He ran, wounded and exhausted, to the banks of Er Lake. The wizard followed and hurled a magic bag toward the lake. The bag made the waves of the lake surge to an enormous height and caused the earth to tremble. The hunter lost his footing on the bank and the earthquake sent him tumbling into the waters of the lake. The waves

washed over the hunter and forced him to the bottom, where he turned into a stone mule.

The poor princess waited all that day and through the night for the return of her husband on Yuju Peak. At daybreak, a crow appeared and told her, 'The hunter has sunk to the bottom of the lake and turned into a stone mule. There he will remain forever.'

The princess was so overcome with sadness that she died a few days later. After her death, her sadness became a cloud. Every Winter, the cloud rises and falls on Yuju Peak, spreading out over the edge as if it were looking directly into the bottom of Er Lake. Whenever this cloud appears, the peaceful waters of Er Lake become dark and turbulent. The storm continues until the waters rise high enough for the stone mule to emerge from the bottom of the lake. Then the cloud drifts up again and recedes back over the mountains. In respect for the princess and the hunter, the people of Dali call this cloud 'Lover Cloud'.

The Taoist at Lao Shan

Long ago, in the sacred mountains of China, there lived a group of men and women following Taoism, a religion of China. Through their special practices, these men and women are said to have developed the power to live forever. Many of these men and women lived at Lao Shan, or 'Old Mountain', and it is here that our story takes place . . .

In a small village at the foot of Lao Shan, there lived a man named Wang Qi. Now, Wang Qi was born into a rich family, so he lived an idle and comfortable life, with servants to take care of his every need. Later he married a beautiful and equally rich wife. His life should have been one of satisfaction. Yet, because Wang Qi usually did nothing all day, he grew bored and restless. When he heard that there were Taoists on Lao Shan who had magical powers and knew the secret for immortality, Wang Qi set off to find them. He hoped they would share their secrets with him.

He climbed over mountain peaks and crossed rivers. He scaled high cliffs and travelled through valleys and pastures. The journey was exhausting, but Wang Qi was so happy thinking about the magic powers he would soon possess that he did not give up. Finally, just when he thought he could go no further, Wang Qi reached the peak of Lao Shan. He passed under the gate and entered the mountain temple.

Inside, the temple was dimly lit, and Wang Qi could just make out the figures of statues filling the room. Smoke from the burning incense hurt Wang Qi's eyes and made them fill with tears. Through the haze, Wang Qi saw an old Taoist master sitting in front of the main altar. The master's hair and beard were as white as snow, but his face had no wrinkles and looked like a young man's.

Wang Qi quickly knelt down at his feet and said, 'Master, I have come to learn the secrets of the Tao from you.'

The master looked at him silently for a few moments and then spoke. 'You will have to undergo many hard tasks to learn Taoism. Your past life has been too comfortable and this has spoiled you. It is impossible for you to do this, so just go home.'

Wang Qi was shocked. 'But Master,' he pleaded, 'it is true that my past way of living has made me afraid of hardship, but I sincerely want to learn. Please help me.'

After pondering Wang Qi's words, the master agreed.

At daybreak the next morning, the master gave Wang Qi an axe. 'From today,' he ordered, 'you must go every day with the other disciples to collect firewood. Remember, don't be lazy!'

And so, in this way, one month quickly passed. Wang Qi was so worn out from his daily tasks that he barely had enough strength to get out of his bed in the morning. In addition, he constantly had pain in his lower back and legs from the strain of the work. He had blisters on his feet which turned into thick calluses. Fed up with his exhausting work, Wang Qi said to himself, 'I have been here for a month and I haven't once seen my master use any magical powers. What is the use of collecting firewood? I would rather go home.'

That evening, Wang Qi and the other disciples were invited to their master's room for a meal. When they arrived, the master and two mysterious guests were sitting in the centre of the room, happily drinking and chatting. Because the room had no lamps, it soon grew very dark. The master took a piece of paper, cut out a round circle with a pair of scissors and hung it on the wall. Suddenly, the round circle began to glow like the moon and the room became filled with moonlight. The disciples and Wang Qi were greatly impressed.

One of the guests gave the disciples a bottle of wine. Even though the disciples drank many glasses, the bottle was always full.

Then, with a shout of joy, one of the guests threw his chopsticks at the moon. In the next moment a beautiful woman stepped out of the moon and said, 'I am Chang E, and I live on the moon. I will sing and dance to welcome you here tonight.'

Wang Qi could not believe it. Here was the immortal Chang E singing for them in his master's room!

After Chang E had finished her lovely song, she vanished. Then the master suggested, 'Why don't we go and drink in the Moon Palace?' Inviting his two guests to join him, the master jumped into the moon circle and disappeared. His two guests quickly joined him, leaving the astonished disciples alone. They continued to drink from the endless bottle of wine, talking excitedly about what they had seen.

After some time, the moonlight from the circle began to dim. Soon, the master reappeared in the room, as if out

of thin air. The 'moon' was now just a circle of paper on the wall. Returning to his room, Wang Qi thought, 'My master really does have magical powers. I will stay and return home after I become an immortal.'

Another month passed, with Wang Qi still collecting firewood every day. The master didn't display any more magical powers, nor did he offer to teach any to Wang Qi. Wang Qi became more and more disheartened, until finally he decided he'd had enough. Approaching the old Taoist master he said, 'I've come to say goodbye. I'm tired of working like a slave!'

But the master only looked at him and laughed. 'I already said the hardship would be too much for you. And since you are so determined, you can leave Lao Shan tomorrow morning.'

Wang Qi was furious. 'I have collected firewood every day for two months, and you haven't taught me any Taoist magic! What was the point of all my work?'

The master became very serious. 'What do you want to learn?' he asked.

Wang Qi thought for a while and replied, 'I saw you disappear through the wall the other night. I want to learn that.'

The Taoist agreed and led him to a wall. 'I will give you a magical formula,' he told Wang Qi. 'Read it silently, and then you'll be able to step through the wall.'

The master gave Wang Qi a piece of paper with ancient Chinese characters on it. Wang Qi read the formula and walked towards the wall. But at the last moment he stopped, scared that he would hit it.

'Don't hesitate!' the master shouted at him. 'Keep your head down and walk quickly, otherwise you cannot go through the wall.'

Wang Qi took a few steps backwards and re-read the formula. Then he dashed towards the wall and appeared out the other side.

He ran back into the room, jumping up and down with excitement. 'I can go through walls!' he exclaimed. 'I am an immortal now!' Then he knelt down and thanked his master.

The Taoist master warned him, 'Remember, after you return home, you have to treat this magic with respect. Don't show off, otherwise you'll destroy the formula and it won't work.'

Wang Qi hastily agreed. Then the master said, 'Here is some money for your hard work. Hurry and leave now so that you can reach home before nightfall.'

Wang Qi quickly forgot the stern warning from his master. After he returned home, he bragged to everyone that he had the power to pass through walls. His wife reproached him. 'Why are you boasting to everyone? You'd be better off to study hard or do some good for others.'

But Wang Qi was puffed up with his own importance. 'Don't you believe I have magical powers?' he said. 'I will show you how I can walk through walls!' He took out the Taoist magic formula, read it and dashed towards the wall. He hit the wall at full force, and fell down on the ground. His head throbbed painfully, and on his forehead was a large, tender lump.

Embarrassed and angry, Wang Qi sat on the floor, cradling his swollen forehead, while his wife stood laughing.

'That Taoist rascal,' he cried. 'He tricked me!'

Agudengba and the Merchant

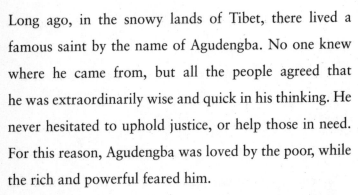

Long ago, in the snowy lands of Tibet, there lived a famous saint by the name of Agudengba. No one knew where he came from, but all the people agreed that he was extraordinarily wise and quick in his thinking. He never hesitated to uphold justice, or help those in need. For this reason, Agudengba was loved by the poor, while the rich and powerful feared him.

In the marketplace at Lhasa, there was a dishonest merchant who sold fake antiques to unsuspecting villagers. This merchant made an enormous profit, for he bought his pieces for a small amount and sold them at high prices.

Agudengba heard about the merchant and decided to teach him a lesson. Carrying a kettle filled with boiling hot tea, Agudengba went behind the merchant's stall. Then he blew a small whistle and waited. The merchant went to investigate, only to find Agudengba sitting on the ground, pouring himself a cup of tea from the kettle.

'Did you hear that whistling earlier? What was that?' asked the merchant.

'Oh, that was just the noise of my kettle boiling. My tea is ready,' said Agudengba.

The merchant was astonished. 'What do you mean? There's no fire here,' he said.

'I don't need a fire,' explained Agudengba. 'You see, this kettle can boil water or tea without fire. Just see for yourself.' And Agudengba showed the merchant his steaming cup of tea.

The merchant was delighted. 'Really? I've never seen the

likes of this!' he exclaimed. Agudengba listened patiently while the merchant made all kinds of offers for the kettle. In the end, the merchant paid fifty taels of silver and one horse for Agudengba's kettle. Agudengba then went and distributed the money to the poor, giving them the horse as well.

Of course, the kettle didn't work and the merchant was furious when he realised he'd been cheated. He swore he would have his revenge on Agudengba. The next day, the merchant saw Agudengba again in the marketplace. He shouted his name and dashed towards him. Agudengba, however, was not worried and casually stepped into a nearby temple.

The entrance to the temple was lined with many pairs of boots belonging to the monks who were inside. Agudengba knelt down at the gate and took out a knife. He picked up one of the boots and cut open the sole.

The merchant found Agudengba and waved his fist at him. 'Liar!' he yelled. 'That kettle doesn't work at all. How dare you cheat me out of my money?'

Agudengba looked surprised, insisting that the kettle had worked for him.

'I demand you return my silver and my horse immediately!' shouted the merchant.

'Of course,' said Agudengba. 'I'll return your money at once. However, the silver and the horse are at my house and I'll have to return home to fetch them. Right now, I have this business to take care of and cannot leave until it is finished.'

The merchant noticed Agudengba was holding some boots. Curious, he asked, 'What are you doing?'

'The head monk assigned me this work,' replied Agudengba. 'If I cut the soles off each of these boots, I will get a handsome reward.'

The merchant's eyes flashed with greed as soon as he heard the word 'reward'. 'Leave this job to me,' he told Agudengba. 'Then you can go home and collect my money while I cut the soles off these boots for you. Hurry now!'

He took out a knife from his bag and knelt down,

busily cutting into the boots. Agudengba stood up and pretended to leave.

Before long, the monks filed out of the temple. When they saw that the soles of their boots were strewn along the ground, they became very angry. They grabbed hold of the bewildered merchant and started to hit him with their boots. Cowering and ashamed, he ran away through the marketplace.

The wounded merchant was even more determined to make Agudengba suffer for what had happened to him. He found Agudengba standing under the canopy of a fruit shop.

'I was beaten because of you!' he roared, grabbing Agudengba by the collar. 'And where is my silver and my horse?'

Seeing the merchant's swollen face, Agudengba almost chuckled to himself, but then pretended to be afraid. 'My lord,' he begged, 'please don't be angry. I didn't know this would happen. That monk must have lied to me!'

The merchant glared at Agudengba suspiciously.

'Truly,' Agudengba continued, 'I ran home to fetch your silver and your horse, but I was delayed by something else.'

'And what was that?' asked the merchant

Agudengba pointed at a tall, wooden pole beside him. 'See,' he said, 'I've been told to guard this pole. It's holding up the canopy of this shop. If you can guard the pole for me, I will go back home immediately and fetch your money and horse. That is, if you still trust me enough to let me go.'

The merchant looked at the wooden pole and thought, 'It's not part of a temple, so I don't have to worry about being beaten by monks. And once he returns, I can get my money and horse.' So the merchant said, 'All right, I will guard this pole for you. Go ahead, but this time you must bring them back immediately!'

Agudengba thanked him and turned to leave. 'Oh, just one more thing,' he said. 'If you see the pole swaying, then it's about to fall. You must shout, "The canopy is falling" as loud as you can to warn the shopkeeper.'

The merchant agreed and watched Agudengba walk away.

Standing next to the wooden pole, the merchant looked up at the canopy. After a long time, he began to feel a little dizzy. Suddenly, a cloud passed over the sun, causing a shadow to move across the pole. The merchant thought the pole was about to fall and shouted, 'Help! The canopy is falling! The canopy is falling!'

The shopkeeper ran towards him, but saw nothing wrong with his canopy. He thought the merchant was trying to fool him and shouted for his assistants to deal with this troublemaker. They pushed the merchant into the street and started throwing old fruit at him. Covered in rotten pulp, the merchant ran down the street. He knew that he'd been fooled once more by Agudengba, yet he had learned his lesson and swore never to cheat others in business again.

The Red Pearls

Long ago, in a small forest cottage deep in the mountains, there lived a young woodcutter named Liu Hai. Every day, Liu Hai chopped wood in the forest and then journeyed to the market in town, where he sold the firewood for a small amount. In this way, Liu Hai provided for himself and his elderly mother. Liu Hai worked from first light in the morning to late at night to give his mother a comfortable life, for she was blind and her health was poor.

One morning, Liu Hai went as usual into the mountain to chop firewood. After walking a short distance, he spotted a large, dead tree with many branches. 'Aha!' he thought to himself. 'This tree will be easy to chop for firewood.'

Liu Hai lifted his axe high above his head and set his aim on the nearest branch. Just as he was ready to bring down his axe, the branch broke off the tree and fell to the ground by itself. Liu Hai was a little frightened, but again approached the tree with his axe. But each time that Liu Hai raised his axe, another branch would fall to the ground. Soon, there was only a pile of firewood where the tree used to be. 'What strange luck!' thought Liu Hai to himself, but he quickly bound the dry wood with rope and lifted the load onto his back.

On his way home, Liu Hai heard footsteps behind him. He turned around and saw a young lady coming down the path. Being shy by nature, Liu Hai continued walking and sped up his steps. But the girl only walked faster and followed him all the way to his house.

At the entrance, Liu Hai turned around and looked at the strange girl. 'Who are you?' he asked. 'Why are you following me from the forest?'

The girl smiled at him and said, 'My name is Ninth Sister. I am very thirsty and would like to have a drink of water.'

Liu Hai went into his house and brought her a bowl of water. Ninth Sister quickly finished her drink and, without waiting to be invited, she walked past Liu Hai into his house.

Liu Hai followed, shocked by her boldness. 'What are you doing?' he demanded. 'Why are you in my house?'

But Ninth Sister ignored him and knelt down by the bedside of Liu Hai's mother. 'I know that you are blind and can't see anything,' she said softly, 'but I can help you.'

Comforted by the gentle tone of Ninth Sister's voice, Liu Hai's mother sat up in her bed. Ninth Sister took out a string of shining red pearls and swung it to and fro in front of the old woman's eyes. Miraculously, her blindness was cured. Blinking in disbelief, she looked at

Liu Hai and exclaimed happily, 'Son, I am able to see!' Then she turned to look at Ninth Sister. 'But who are you and where do you come from?'

'I am a homeless girl and I live alone,' replied Ninth Sister. 'I often see Brother Liu chopping firewood in the mountain forest. I know that he is generous and has a good heart. Forgive my boldness, but I want to marry him and live here as your daughter-in-law.'

When Liu Hai heard this, he was greatly shocked. 'No, no,' he said, shaking his head. 'I am poor, we don't have much money. I have to look after my mother. You will only suffer if you become my wife.'

But Ninth Sister would not be put off. 'I find you so handsome, and I already know that you are kind-hearted and a hard worker. You are the man I wish to marry.'

Taken aback, Liu Hai blushed. He also liked this beautiful and forthright strange lady. He turned to ask his mother, but his mother was already out of bed, welcoming Ninth sister as her future daughter-in-law. So Liu Hai and Ninth Sister were married that day, accompanied by

Liu Hai's mother. Liu Hai continued to sell firewood in the market and Ninth Sister stayed at home, taking care of Liu Hai's mother.

One morning, when Ninth Sister had gone to the market to buy some rice, Liu Hai's mother heard someone outside calling for help. Opening the door, she saw an old, blind beggar, collapsed on their doorstep. She helped him sit up, and the old beggar pointed to his eyes, saying how terrible it was that he could not see. Liu Hai's mother remembered that Ninth Sister had used the red pearls to cure her blindness, so she fetched the pearls and held them in front of the old beggar's eyes.

But the old beggar was only pretending to be blind, and he snatched the string of pearls from her hand. Laughing with glee, he made to run away when Ninth Sister returned home. Seeing the old man with her pearls, she ran towards him and caught him, but the old man was strong and pushed Ninth Sister away. Then he magically transformed into a large, golden toad and jumped high above their heads. A strong gust of wind blew past the cottage and the toad disappeared into the sky.

Ninth Sister cried out in horror. 'Mother,' she wept, 'that toad has stolen my pearls and now I can no longer live here with you and Liu Hai!' She dashed down the pathway and ran into the mountains.

When Liu Hai returned home from the market, his mother told him what had happened. Liu Hai could hardly believe what he heard, but he knew he had to find Ninth Sister and help her.

'Don't worry,' he said. 'I will find Ninth Sister and her pearls and bring them back!' Then he picked up his walking stick and set off into the mountains.

As he journeyed in the forest, Liu Hai called out to Ninth Sister, but he heard no response. Soon he came across the entrance of a cave, where he saw a group of beautiful women sitting inside. And there amongst them was Ninth Sister! Liu Hai happily ran towards her and grasped her hands.

'Why are you sitting here in this cave?' he asked. 'Come home with me!'

Ninth Sister's eyes filled with tears. 'Now I must tell you the truth,' she said. 'These are my sisters and we are fox spirits. I studied the Tao for thousands of years to obtain those magical pearls. The pearls are my life energy and allow me to stay in the human world. Without them, I will return to my original form.'

Ninth Sister began to cry, but Liu Hai consoled her. 'Even if you were a fox, I would still love you,' he said. 'I will find the golden toad and bring back your pearls!'

Suddenly, Liu Hai's walking stick began to shimmer and a voice started speaking. 'I am the god of your walking stick,' it said. 'I have listened to your story and I can help you by guiding you to the cave of the golden toad.'

The sisters cheered. Liu Hai smiled at Ninth Sister. 'With the help of my god,' he said, 'we will find the golden toad and recover your pearls.'

By this time the toad was back in his small mountain cave, revelling in his new-found treasure. He held the shiny pearls up to his mouth. 'If I swallow these pearls,'

he thought to himself, 'I will become immortal, the greatest among all toads!'

But just then he heard the sound of Liu Hai and the sisters approaching. Hopping outside, he threw some magical coins into the sky above them. The coins flew up into the air and became heavy stones as they fell. The sisters saw the stones and used their magical sleeves as a shield so the stones bounced harmlessly to the ground. But while they were busy protecting themselves, the golden toad quickly swallowed the string of pearls.

Liu Hai saw what had happened and threw his walking stick at the toad. In midair, the shimmering stick transformed into a large boa constrictor. The boa wrapped itself around the golden toad and began to choke him, forcing the pearls out of his mouth.

Ninth Sister rushed over and grabbed her shining string of pearls. She was immediately filled with new energy. The boa fell to the ground and changed back into a stick, while the golden toad limped weakly away, never to bother them again.

All the sisters sang and danced around Liu Hai and Ninth Sister, congratulating them on their victory. Picking up his magic walking stick, Liu Hai held out his hand and led Ninth Sister back home to their small cottage, where they lived happily ever after.

Zhao Shu Tun and the Kingdom of Peacocks

In an ancient kingdom near the tropical jungles of southern China, there was a brave, handsome prince by the name of Zhao Shu Tun. Adventurous by nature, he often went hunting in the forest alone.

One day, Zhao left at dawn to travel to a sacred lake. Nearing the lake, he heard the laughter of young girls, but this laughter sounded like the ringing of tiny bells. Intrigued, Zhao peered through the trees and saw seven beautiful girls bathing in the lake. Zhao couldn't imagine where the seven girls had come from, so he hid in the reeds and watched.

Suddenly, one of the girls saw Zhao. She cried out to her companions and the seven girls quickly ran ashore and dressed themselves in colourful clothes made of feathers. Then they changed into seven peahens and flew up into the sky.

Zhao was amazed. He stood up and called out to the sacred dragon that guarded the lake. The surface of the lake swelled up and down as the dragon emerged from the waters.

'Dragon, who are those seven maidens and where do they come from?' asked Zhao.

'Ah,' the sacred dragon answered. 'They are the seven princesses from the Kingdom of Peacocks. Every seven days they come to this lake to bathe.'

'And of the seven princesses,' Zhao asked, 'who is the most beautiful?'

'The youngest princess,' replied the dragon. 'Her name is Nan Nuo Na. She is by far the most beautiful of them all.'

Zhao decided to wait for the seven peahen princesses to return. He made a small tree-house out of bamboo where he could watch the maidens, unobserved. After seven days, the princesses returned. One by one, they took off their feather clothes and changed into seven young girls. Watching from his tree house, Zhao saw that the youngest princess was indeed the most beautiful.

Silently, Zhao climbed down from the tree and slipped through the reeds by the shore. He took Nan's feather clothes and returned back to his tree-house. Up in the branches, he began to sing. The song drifted towards the lake, causing the seven princesses to become alarmed and return to shore. Soon, six peahens took off into the sky.

But Nan couldn't find her clothes and had to hide in the reeds. She saw Zhao walking towards her dressed like a hunter and cried out fearfully, 'Who are you? Go away!'

Zhao was about to answer her when the six peahen princesses landed on the ground. They had seen Zhao approaching their sister and had returned to save her.

But Zhao stood firmly between them and Nan, and refused to return her clothes or let her go. Unable to fight him, the six peahen princesses reluctantly flew off to tell their father what had happened.

Zhao took off his cloak and handed it to Nan. 'Don't be afraid,' he said gently. 'I mean you no harm. My name is Zhao Shu Tun, and I am the prince of this kingdom. Please come and sit with me so we can talk.'

Now, Nan had already heard of Zhao, for he was famous throughout the lands of the south, so she put on Zhao's cloak and stood up from the reeds. As they sat talking, Zhao became friendlier and Nan no longer felt afraid. She admired his honesty and kind manner.

As the afternoon continued, Nan told Zhao that she had never felt as happy as she did in that moment. Zhao was overjoyed and confessed his love for her. 'Marry me and come to live in my kingdom,' he asked. Nan agreed, and together they returned to Zhao's palace.

The wedding ceremony of Zhao Shu Tun and Nan Nuo Na was a royal event. Musicians from far away arrived with brass instruments and drums, filling the city with the sounds of celebration. The women at court wore their most elaborate jewellery, and the men dressed in silk vests and trousers. From their carriage on top of an elephant, the royal couple paraded through the entire city, accepting congratulations from all the people in the kingdom.

Meanwhile, at the Kingdom of Peacocks, King Ba Tu An was very angry when he heard from his six daughters that Nan had been abducted by a hunter. The news spread throughout the kingdom, and the order was given to prepare for war. Believing that his daughter was in grave danger, King Ba ordered his army to attack the kingdom where the hunter lived and rescue Princess Nan.

Soon King Ba's army reached the border of Prince Zhao's kingdom. When news reached the prince that his kingdom was under attack, he decided to lead his army onto the battlefield.

'I must protect the kingdom,' he said to Nan. 'Stay here, where it is safe, and I will return as soon as we have defeated the invaders.'

But Princess Nan was not safe. As soon as Prince Zhao left, the court wizards went to find Nan's father-in-law, the king.

'Princess Nan is a stranger to us,' they said. 'She doesn't belong here. She will bring us bad fortune. This war is evidence! The only way heaven will protect us is if we sacrifice her to the gods of this land.'

Worried by the sudden war raging at his borders, the king accepted what the court wizards said and had Princess Nan arrested. He gave the order for her to be put to death.

Princess Nan begged the king to wait for the return of her husband, but he refused. 'Then at least let me wear my feather clothes again,' she pleaded. The king agreed and handed over her clothes. Princess Nan quickly put on the feather garments and, to the surprise of everyone present, transformed into a peahen. Then she flew away from her captors towards the Kingdom of Peacocks.

At the battlefield, Prince Zhao fought bravely alongside his soldiers. Within a day, the invaders had retreated and Zhao claimed victory for his kingdom. It was only afterwards that he learned the invaders had come from the Kingdom of Peacocks. He was greatly distressed and swiftly mounted his horse to return home.

When he arrived, he was told that Nan had flown away. He quickly rode to the sacred lake and called forth the dragon. 'Tell me what happened to Princess Nan,' he demanded.

'The princess is gone,' the dragon replied. 'But before she flew back home, she gave me this gold bracelet. Take it, for it will help you find her.'

Zhao took the bracelet and thanked the dragon.

'Wait,' said the dragon. 'I will also give you a bottle of medicine and a magic arrow, for you will need these as well.'

With the gifts from the dragon tucked safely in his pocket, Prince Zhao set off for the Kingdom of Peacocks.

After climbing many mountains and crossing countless rivers, he finally reached the kingdom. He stopped his horse to rest and saw a young girl filling up a water pot from a well. 'Where does Princess Nan Nuo Na live?' he asked her.

'I am her maid,' the girl said. 'I am drawing this water for her bath. Why do you want to know where she is?'

'I have come here to bless her,' Zhao replied, and he dropped the gold bracelet into the pot.

While Princess Nan was having her bath, she saw the gold bracelet in her maid's pot. 'Where did you get this?' she asked excitedly. On hearing the maid's description of the man at the well, Nan clapped her hands and exclaimed, 'It is Zhao! He has come to find me at last!' She ran to tell her parents the news.

Since the battle, King Ba had learned that the hunter who abducted his daughter was not a hunter at all, but the prince of a distant kingdom. He now regretted invading Prince Zhao's kingdom and ordered that Zhao be brought to the royal palace.

'Prince Zhao,' said King Ba, 'although you are already married to Princess Nan in your kingdom, you must obey the laws of this kingdom and pass two tests. The tests will prove whether you have strength and sincerity. If you succeed, I will allow you to be with Princess Nan.'

Prince Zhao quickly agreed.

King Ba ordered his men to make an iron wall, a stone wall and a wooden wall, one in front of the other. 'If you can shoot through these walls,' King Ba told Zhao, 'I will recognise you as my son-in-law.'

Zhao mounted his horse and rode out a far distance from the walls. Then, galloping at great speed, he took out the dragon's magic arrow and shot it from his bow. The arrow hit the first wall with such force that all three walls cracked. The people cheered at Zhao's display of strength.

King Ba, however, was not convinced. He asked his men to construct a tent and cut a thousand small holes in the walls. King Ba then asked Princess Nan and nine hundred and ninety-nine other girls to enter the tent and stick their ring finger through the holes. He told Zhao, 'If you cannot find the finger that belongs to my daughter, then you should immediately return to your kingdom.'

As Prince Zhao approached the tent, he took out the dragon's bottle of medicine. He placed one drop of medicine on each of the girls' ring fingers. Suddenly, one of the rings began to glow with a white light. Zhao knew this was the finger of the princess. With joy, he shouted, 'I found her!' and cut open the tent with his knife. Princess Nan fell happily into his arms.

That night there was a grand celebration in the Kingdom of Peacocks. Prince Zhao's parents were invited and the two kingdoms declared peace and friendship to each other. All who attended marvelled at the bravery and wisdom of Prince Zhao, and the beauty and courage of Princess Nan. They wished them long life and happiness, forever and ever.

Panhu, the Dragon Dog

A Yao Tale

A long time ago, in the tropical forests of southern China, there lived a king by the name of Gaoxin. King Gaoxin was a noble ruler who was much respected by his people, but his kingdom was constantly under attack from neighbouring kingdoms. As a result, King Gaoxin was often unwell, for he worried greatly about the fate of his people.

One morning, King Gaoxin woke up with great pain in his right ear. He immediately called for his doctor, for the pain was so severe that the poor king could not lift his head from his pillow.

The doctor knelt down beside the bed and examined the king's ear. To his surprise, he found a large caterpillar resting inside.

'My lord,' said the doctor, 'I've found the cause of your earache. You have a large caterpillar in your ear! I'll remove it at once.'

As the king wondered how a caterpillar had managed to crawl into his ear, the doctor swiftly removed the caterpillar and placed it on a plate by the king's bed. The caterpillar's body shimmered as if covered in gold and its bristles shone with all the colours of the rainbow.

'Interesting,' said the doctor, as he stood up to take the plate away.

'Wait!' King Gaoxin shouted. 'This caterpillar is indeed interesting, so I'll keep it here, just to see what happens to it.'

King Gaoxin ordered his men to bring leaves and plants to feed the caterpillar. They placed the food on the plate and covered it with a serving lid. Then they took the plate to the room next to the king's.

For seven days and seven nights, King Gaoxin was busy with the affairs of his kingdom, and he forgot about the unusual caterpillar. Then, on the morning of the eighth day, the king remembered his strange earache and ordered one of his servants to bring the caterpillar to him.

But when the servant tried to lift the plate, he found he was not strong enough, for the plate was extremely heavy. 'My lord,' he cried, 'something has happened to the caterpillar. I cannot lift the plate!'

'What do you mean?' said the king as he entered the room. 'It's just a tiny caterpillar.' With those words, the king lifted the lid and saw not a caterpillar, but a huge dog! The dog was as big as a grown man and its fur shimmered like silk. It jumped down from the plate and bowed its head, as if presenting itself to the king. King Gaoxin was delighted and decided to name the dog Panhu, or Dragon Dog.

Panhu became the king's companion and followed the king wherever he went. He soon became known as a good hunter and a fearless warrior, and tales of his bravery were told throughout the kingdom. Even though Panhu was only a dog, he enjoyed all the favours of King Gaoxin's court, and his life was happy indeed.

Then, one day, an enemy army invaded the kingdom. The king summoned his general and all his ministers to prepare for war.

'The enemy's army is commanded by a fierce general,' counselled the king's ministers. 'We must kill him if we are to be victorious.'

'Very well,' announced the king. 'Whoever kills the general and brings me his sword as proof shall be rewarded with the hand of my third daughter in marriage.'

After the king finished speaking there was silence. No one dared volunteer for the task of killing the general; they were too terrified. Yet Panhu heard what the king had said and silently left the court, unnoticed by the others.

That very afternoon, Panhu arrived at the camp of the enemy and hid in the general's tent. As the sky grew dark and the general lay down to sleep, Panhu attacked him. The general was no match for Panhu's great strength and size. With no one to stop him, Panhu took the general's sword in his mouth, slipped out of the general's tent and headed back to King Gaoxin's kingdom.

The next morning, the enemy army discovered that their leader was dead and immediately surrendered.

When the king heard of his victory, he was greatly surprised, for none of his men had taken up his challenge. As he sat pondering the news on his throne, Panhu appeared, carrying the general's sword in his mouth. 'Panhu!' cried the king. 'It is you who have defeated the enemy.'

Panhu laid the sword at the king's feet and sat waiting, as if in expectation.

King Gaoxin didn't know what to do. He remembered his promise to give his third daughter in marriage to the one who brought him the general's sword, but Panhu was a dog, not a man. How could he marry his beloved daughter to a dog? Yet King Gaoxin was a man of his word, and he dared not go back on his promise.

Suddenly, as if sensing the king's dilemma, Panhu began to speak. 'My lord,' he said, 'I know you are worried, because you cannot marry your third daughter to a dog. But if you make a huge bell out of gold and keep me under it for seven days and seven nights, I will turn into a man. Then I can marry your daughter the princess, and become your son-in-law.'

King Gaoxin was delighted to hear Panhu's solution. He opened up his treasury to his blacksmiths and told them to take as much gold as they needed to make a giant bell.

The royal blacksmiths worked for three days and three nights, and finally the golden bell was finished. Panhu then instructed the blacksmiths to create a door in the side.

When it was completed, Panhu entered the bell. 'Make sure that you only open this door after seven days and seven nights,' he said, before the door was shut firmly behind him.

Now, the third daughter of King Gaoxin heard about her betrothal to Panhu and the magic instructions that had been given to the king. She knew that the royal blacksmiths had made a golden bell, and that Panhu was inside it. 'Will he really turn into a man?' she wondered. 'What will he be like?'

The princess thought about Panhu day and night. Finally, after six days, her curiosity was so great that she asked her lady-in-waiting to check on him.

The lady-in-waiting walked around and around the giant bell and saw that it was solid and smooth, without a single crack. She brought her eye close to the edges of the door, straining to catch a glimpse of Panhu, but she could not see anything. At last, she gave up and returned to the princess.

When the princess heard that the giant bell was impenetrable, she began to worry. What if something had happened to Panhu? What if he could not breathe?

She quickly ran to the bell and knocked three times on its hard surface. 'Panhu! Panhu!' she shouted, but there

was no answer. She put her ear against the bell's surface, but all was silent. 'Oh no!' she thought. 'My future husband has died of hunger!' Without waiting another second, she pulled open the door in the bell.

Inside the bell was a tall and handsome man, with hair like silk that shone with all the colours of the rainbow.

'Greetings, Princess,' said the man. 'I am Panhu. My transformation is not complete, but because you have opened this bell early, I must remain this way for ever.'

The princess quickly apologised for her rashness and pleaded for forgiveness, yet Panhu was not angry with her. He offered his hand to the princess and together they left the giant bell.

When King Gaoxin saw Panhu's transformation, he was delighted. He gave Panhu the title 'Duke of Pan' because of his past bravery. The Duke of Pan and the princess were married, and the entire kingdom came to celebrate the royal wedding.

Soon after the wedding, the newlyweds left the palace to live a simple, normal life in the countryside. The Duke of Pan was happy to be hunting again in the forest, and the princess planted crops of vegetables in their garden. After twelve years had passed, they had a family of six boys and six girls.

These twelve children were the twelve original ancestors of the Yao people. Because the Duke of Pan was the father of the original ancestors, the Yao people have a dog as their symbol, to pay tribute to Panhu. Every twelve years, they carry out a sacred ceremony for the Duke of Pan, where they beat drums and sing songs of remembrance. This festival is filled with singing and dancing, and is still a great ceremony for the Yao people in China today.

Ashima

A Yi Tale

High up in a mountain village in the province of Sichuan, there lived a family with one son and one daughter. The son's name was Ahei, and the daughter's name was Ashima. Ahei was as strong as a forest pine, and he excelled at horse riding, archery and singing. His sister, Ashima, was as beautiful as a flower, and was known for her fine embroidery and weaving skills. Everyone agreed that the family was blessed to have such a wonderful son and daughter.

As Ashima grew up, all the young men in the village wanted to marry her. Her parents told her that she could choose a husband for herself.

'I only want to marry someone who is honest and hardworking,' Ashima told them.

A rich landlord called Rebulaba lived at the foot of the mountain with his son, Azhi. Rebulaba had heard of Ashima's beauty and thought she would make a fine wife for his son. He asked the village matchmaker to propose on his son's behalf. 'Tell the family that I have mountains of treasures and sheep and cattle,' he said. 'Ashima will never have to worry if she marries into a family like this.'

The matchmaker left to find Ashima's parents, and told them what Rebulaba had said. 'If Ashima agrees to this marriage, then she will lead a rich and carefree life,' he promised them.

'That is true,' replied her mother, 'but this landlord is from the valley and doesn't know our ways. It is up to Ashima to decide, so we must wait for her.'

Ashima returned home and listened to the matchmaker's proposal, including the description of Rebulaba's wealth. Abruptly, she stood up and said angrily, 'I will never marry into such a family! They are cruel and lazy. They only have wealth because they take money from the farmers who work for them.'

The matchmaker was shocked by Ashima's words and asked, 'Would you rather marry someone poor and suffer for the rest of your life?'

Ashima nodded. 'I'd rather have hardship,' she answered, 'than the company of Rebulaba's family.'

Then she walked out of the room, leaving the confused matchmaker alone with her parents, who refused to say another word about the subject. Having failed in his task, the matchmaker had no option but to leave.

When Rebulaba heard that Ashima had rejected his proposal, he was furious. He decided to kidnap Ashima so she would be forced to marry his son. He waited for a time when Ashima's brother was away herding cattle, then sent his servants to the house. Ashima and her parents were no match for Rebulaba's men, and Ashima agreed to go without a struggle.

'Send Ahei to save me!' she told her parents as she was being led away.

That night, Ahei dreamt that his parents were calling him because their house had been washed away by a flood. When he woke the next morning, he quickly gathered together his herd and started the trek back home.

As soon as he entered the village, his neighbors ran up and told him what had happened. Ahei found his parents at home, still crying over the fate of Ashima. 'Don't worry,' he assured them. 'I will bring Ashima back.' Grabbing his bow and arrows, Ahei saddled his horse and galloped down the mountain towards the valley.

Meanwhile, Ashima was being held like a prisoner in Rebulaba's home. His son, Azhi, tried to win her over with gifts. 'All these jewels and gold are yours,' he said, smiling his monkey-like grin. 'And I can get you even more if you want. Surely these will satisfy you?'

But Ashima refused to look at them. 'Your treasures

are rubbish to me,' she said. 'Stop wasting your time and let me go!'

Azhi's face flushed red with shame and he ran out of the room. Soon Rebubala appeared in the doorway.

'How dare you refuse to marry my son,' he threatened. 'You are in my house now and must obey me, or I will have you beaten!'

But Ashima stood firm. 'Go ahead and kill me if you wish,' she said. 'I would rather die than marry your son!'

Rebulaba flew into a rage and had Ashima locked in the dungeon.

The next day, Ahei arrived at Rebulaba's house. Riding around the outer walls, he shouted Ashima's name. Finally, he heard her whistle in response and knew that she was inside. He dismounted from his horse at the main gate and demanded Ashima's release.

'Let my sister go,' he shouted, 'or I'll break down your gate!'

Now, both Rebulaba and Azhi were afraid of Ahei, so they tried to trick him. Azhi climbed to the top of a wall and shouted, 'We will have a singing contest. If you win, I will let you in.'

Ahei agreed, and Azhi began to sing one of the songs from his valley. When he had finished, Ahei sang a song from his village. Trading song for song, both of them sang for hours. Finally, Azhi had exhausted all the songs he knew, while Ahei kept singing. Admitting defeat, Azhi opened the gate and let Ahei in.

Immediately, Rebulaba appeared. 'Wait!' he demanded. 'Before you enter into my house, we must have a contest. If you chop down more trees and plant more seeds than both Azhi and I, then you may enter.'

Ahei knew that this was unfair, but he agreed. Wielding his axe, Ahei brought down three trees in a row with one swing. Then he sowed three strips of land. Meanwhile, Rebulaba and Azhi had only brought down one tree and sowed one strip of land before they were overcome with exhaustion. They sat on the ground, too tired to continue the challenge.

'You've lost this contest as well,' said Ahei, 'so keep

your bargain and let Ashima go.'

'Okay, okay,' said Rebulaba, still panting for breath. Then he released Ashima. She ran to embrace her brother and the two prepared to leave.

'Wait!' Rebulaba said suddenly. 'It's dark already, and you cannot both travel on the one horse. Stay for one night, and in the morning I'll give you another horse so you can return home.'

Ashima and Ahei looked at one another, for they did not trust Rebulaba, but they knew it was impossible to journey up the mountain in the dark. They agreed to stay the night and took a room upstairs.

As soon as Ashima and Ahei were asleep, Rebulaba released three tigers into their room, hoping the tigers would eat them. But Ahei was only pretending to sleep, and he shot three arrows in a row, killing the tigers.

The next morning, he confronted Rebulaba. 'You are as cold-blooded as your tigers,' he said. 'You have done nothing but try to trick us. Ashima and I are leaving this minute!'

Ahei led his sister to the gate, but as soon as he stepped through, Rebulaba's servants grabbed Ashima and slammed it shut, bolting the wooden door closed.

'Ahei!' she called, pounding on the door. 'He's tricked you again!'

Ahei was furious. 'Rebulaba,' he yelled, 'I won't forgive you this time!' He pulled out his bow and shot three arrows over the gate. One hit the door, another hit the family column and the last hit the family crest.

Rebulaba was horrified; the door, column and crest represented his family's honour. Ahei's arrows would bring them ruin and misfortune. He desperately tried to pull out the arrows, but they wouldn't budge. Then Azhi came to help his father, but he failed as well. Finally, Rebulaba had to open the front gate and beg Ahei to pull out the arrows.

But it was Ashima who walked forward. 'Evil men will never be able to remove these arrows,' she said. Chanting Ahei's name under her breath, she pulled the three arrows out of the wood as easily as if she were picking flowers.

Rebulaba did not dare try to stop Ashima as she walked out of the gate. He watched as the brother and sister left together. But as soon as they were out of sight, he took off on his horse to follow them. He planned to kill Ahei and bring Ashima back to his house.

On the way home, Ahei led his horse and took his sister's hand. 'See?' he smiled. 'Your brother is like a hat that protects you.'

Ashima laughed. 'True,' she said. 'And your sister is like a tree that gives you shade and rest.'

Ahei smiled, but his smile faded when they reached the river. The sky had grown dark as they walked and soon heavy drops of rain were falling, causing the waters of the river to spill over the banks.

'What shall we do?' asked Ashima. She glanced around her and saw Rebulaba approaching swiftly on his horse. With great speed, he attacked Ahei and knocked him to the ground. Then he caught Ashima with his whip, so she could not run away. Before Ahei could recover, Rebulaba had drawn his sword and was about to kill him.

'No!' Ashima cried. She jumped into the raging river, pulling a surprised Rebulaba with her. The swirling current was too strong for the rich landlord, and he drowned.

Ahei ran up and down the banks of the river searching for his sister, but he could see no sign of her. 'Ashima! Ashima!' he cried, when suddenly he heard a voice.

'Ahei! I am calling to you from the sky. My soul has become immortal and I live in the rocks high above you. Do not worry, for I will always be here to answer whenever you call.'

Ahei realised that Ashima had become a god for her sacrifice. He went home saddened, but often returned to the mountaintop to speak to his sister.

'Ashima!' he would shout up at the mountain and wait for her reply. In this way, he always remembered his brave and heroic sister.

Chinese New Year

The New Year, which is called 'Guo Nian' in Chinese, is the most important holiday in China. It marks the end of Winter and the start of Spring. The air is filled with festivities and good cheer, and celebrations last a whole week. During this season, people decorate their homes with red papercuttings and scrolls that say 'Chun Jie', or Spring Festival. Red lanterns hang in parks and temples, and families dressed in red eat Chinese dumplings to celebrate the luck of the New Year.

But the New Year was not always a joyful time of celebration. In fact, long ago, people dreaded the arrival of 'Guo Nian'. There is a famous story of how the New Year came to be what it is today.

In ancient times, there existed a horrible creature in China known as Nian. Nian lived at the bottom of the sea, and was as long as twelve fishing boats put together. A single horn grew out of its head and its body was covered in scales like a fish.

Every year on New Year's Eve, Nian would wake up and leave its underwater home in search of food. These visits brought disaster to all the villages in its path. First, the sea would begin to boil and churn as Nian surfaced from the depths. Then, terrifying floods and earthquakes would begin, for everywhere that Nian travelled, the earth would shake in fear. People and animals fled for their lives, but Nian was too powerful and devoured every living creature that it saw. Finally, before the rising of the morning sun, Nian would return back to the sea to sleep, far away from sunlight and heat, for another three hundred and sixty-five days.

Of course, because of the yearly visits of Nian, the ancient Chinese loathed the coming of the new year. A week before New Year, villages were filled with the cries of people, warning, 'Nian is coming! Nian is coming!' Then the villagers would prepare food and clothing, for they had to abandon their homes to hide high up in the mountains. Only in this way were they safe from the destruction of Nian.

But one New Year's Eve, there was an old woman who refused to leave her home and hide in the mountains. This woman had lost her only son to Nian the previous year, so she was very sad. She was also very old, and did not think her body would make the hard journey up into the mountains. She decided to stay and wait for the arrival of Nian. In her heart, she swore that she would fight the horrible creature, though she had no idea how.

As she was sitting by the fire in her small house, she heard a knock on the door. The old woman was surprised, for the villagers had already left for the mountains, and there was no one around. The knock came again, so the old woman went to the door and opened it.

Standing outside, in the swirling snow and bitterly cold wind, was a beggar. He leaned on a bamboo pole and wore dirty, threadbare clothes. 'Have mercy, kind lady,' he said. 'I've had nothing to eat for days and my clothes are no protection from these Winter winds.'

The old woman was shocked but quickly ushered the beggar into her house. He placed his bamboo pole against the wall and warmed his hands and feet by the fire.

The old woman went into the kitchen and soon came back with a steaming bowl of food. 'Here are some dump-lings I have made,' she said, handing the beggar the bowl and some chopsticks. 'Please pardon this small meal, but I am here by myself and do not have much.'

The beggar was delighted by the sight of the dumplings and quickly ate them, exclaiming all the while, 'Good! Good!' When he had finished, he rested the chopsticks on the top of the bowl and sat back happily in his chair.

'I've been to all the houses in this village,' said the beggar. 'There's no one here but you. Why are there no people around?'

The old woman sighed and said sadly, 'Because it's New Year's Eve. All the people have fled to the mountains. You'd best leave soon as well, for the creature Nian will arrive tonight, and if you are here you will be its feast.'

But the beggar did not seem scared at all. Instead, he laughed loudly and exclaimed, 'Run from Nian? Nian is easy to deal with it. Just wait and see how I defeat it!'

The old woman's eyes opened wide in disbelief. 'What's this?' she said. 'You aren't afraid of Nian? Don't you know how terrible this creature is? It's best that you leave right away for your own safety.'

But the beggar was not frightened by the old woman's warnings. 'No, no, I'll stay,' he insisted. 'I only ask that you give me a large piece of red cloth and two pieces of red paper. And by the way,' he added, 'your dumplings are really delicious. Could you prepare some more for us to eat later tonight?'

Although the old woman was puzzled by the beggar's request, she went to her wardrobe and gave him a large bolt of red cloth. She found two sheets of red paper on her desk and handed these to him as well. Then she returned to the kitchen and began to make more fillings for her tasty dumplings.

The beggar unrolled the bolt of cloth and cut himself a piece large enough for two cloaks. He wrapped the cloth around him, making sure that it covered all his clothing. Then he pasted the two sheets of red paper on the front door of the old woman's house. Picking up his bamboo stick, he left the house and went to stand in the courtyard.

Down by the beach, seawater was already running onto the shore. In the distance, the sea churned and frothed as if a violent storm was rising from its depths. Nian was waking up.

Crashing onto the ground like thunder, Nian landed on the shore. Its vicious eyes were shining and its terrifying mouth hung open as it sped towards the village.

Nian was extremely hungry and was looking for whatever food it could get.

Yet back at the village the old beggar stood unafraid, leaning on his bamboo pole. All of a sudden, the earth began to tremble and he knew that Nian was coming. He reached inside his clothes and struck two flints against his pole. Soon the pole began to burn, and a loud cracking noise filled the air.

The old woman ran outside, for she had never heard such a strange sound. She saw the old beggar wrapped in red cloth, holding high his bamboo pole. From the top of the pole, a shower of crackling sparks shot up into the sky.

Nian also heard the sound. To its ears, the noise was like the crackling of a thousand flashes of lightning. Nian grew angrier and angrier as the noise went on, and roared with all its might, hoping to silence whoever was making such a sound. The old lady heard Nian's roar and ran into her house, convinced that this would be her last night alive.

As the crackling sound became even louder, Nian felt like its head was ready to explode. It sped into the village and saw the old beggar standing in the courtyard, holding a pole from which thousands of tiny suns were exploding. The light pierced Nian's eyes like knives, and Nian howled in response. The red clothes of the beggar and the red paper added to the power of the light, and the noise became so deafening that Nian began to twist around in pain. Finally, Nian retreated back to the sea, not even daring to stop and find food.

The beggar stood laughing as he watched the retreating figure of Nian. 'See?' he said to the old woman when she timidly stepped outside. 'Nian has been frightened away.'

He smiled, then drew the red cloth over his head and promptly disappeared. The old woman realised the beggar was actually a kind-hearted immortal. All that remained of him was a bundle of red cloth and some small bamboo firecrackers on the snowy ground. The old woman picked up his gifts and went inside.

The next day, all the villagers came down from the mountain, expecting to see their houses in ruins. Instead, they saw the village untouched and, even more surprisingly, the old woman was sitting in her courtyard eating dumplings!

As they crowded around the old woman in curiosity, she told them what had happened. Everybody rejoiced to hear that Nian was defeated. The creature had been so frightened that it never dared come out of the sea again.

From that time onwards, people have worn red clothes, hung red paper and lit firecrackers every New Year's Eve.

So remember the next time Chinese New Year comes around, the more noise you make with your firecrackers, the better!

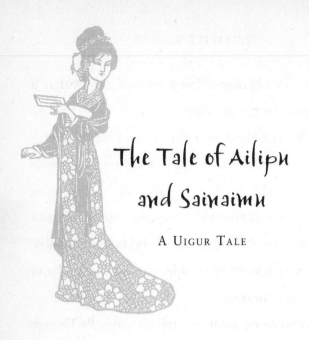

The Tale of Ailipu
and Sainaimu

A Uigur Tale

Long ago in the ancient western lands of China, there
lived a king and queen who ruled over prosperous lands.
In their court, there was also a prime minister who looked
after government affairs.

The prime minister's name was Aishan, and both he
and his wife were good friends of the king and queen. It
so happened that the queen and Aishan's wife were due
to give birth at the same time. The two families decided
that if one child was a boy and the other a girl, then

their children should marry. The king even gave Aishan a golden ring to seal the promise.

Later that year, the queen gave birth to a baby girl, and they called her Sainaimu. The prime minister's wife gave birth to a baby boy, whom they called Ailipu. Both families were very happy with their good fortune, and in the next few years Sainaimu and Ailipu became friends. When the time came, they attended the same school and spent much time together.

One day, however, Ailipu's father became ill. Though the king sent his best physicians, there was nothing anyone could do to help Aishan recover. He died soon afterwards, and both families were overcome with grief. Ailipu and his mother moved to a small house near the outskirts of the capital, and gradually their life became very poor. But Ailipu continued his studies at school, and helped his mother with housework and chores in his spare time.

Sainaimu often went to visit Ailipu at his house. She would help Ailipu's mother with her chores and assist Ailipu with his studies.

For the next ten years, Ailipu and Sainaimu were inseparable. By this time, Ailipu had grown into a handsome young man, and Sainaimu a beautiful young woman. It wasn't long before they realised they had fallen in love. They both knew of their parents' agreement and looked forward to the day when their engagement would be announced.

One day, Sainaimu was walking past the main palace hall when she overheard her parents discussing plans for her future. Hiding behind one of the doors, she listened intently to their conversation.

'The time has come for Sainaimu to marry,' said the queen, 'but she can't marry Ailipu. His family is poor, and it isn't right for a royal princess to marry a poor man.'

The king, however, had misgivings. 'We must remember our promise to Aishan,' he reminded the queen.

But she could not be convinced. 'In that case, we'll forbid Sainaimu from seeing Ailipu. She will soon forget about him and then we won't have to worry about our promise.'

The king thought for a moment, then agreed. 'Fine,' he said. 'From now on, Sainaimu is not allowed out of the palace to see Ailipu.'

When Sainaimu heard this she was so upset she ran to her room and burst into tears.

Her maid Ahe was distressed to see the princess crying. 'What's wrong?' she asked.

'My parents have broken their promise. I am not allowed out of the palace to see Ailipu ever again!' Sainaimu explained.

But Ahe had a plan. 'Tell the king that you must go into town to say goodbye to your teacher,' she said. 'I'm sure he will let you go.'

Sainaimu followed Ahe's suggestion, and the king agreed to let her leave the palace. She went straight to Ailipu's house and quickly told him the news that her parents wanted to cancel their marriage. 'We should run away and elope!' she said.

But Ailipu was worried by such a rash plan. 'Your parents are rulers of this kingdom,' he argued. 'If we run away, they'll have us captured and then punished.' He walked over to a small jewellery box and took out the golden engagement ring with the king's seal. Then he handed it to Sainaimu, saying, 'If you show this to your father, I'm sure he will not stop our marriage.'

As soon as Sainaimu returned to the palace, she presented the engagement ring to her father. 'You are ruler of these lands,' she said. 'As king, you have the duty to keep the promises you have made. If you don't, then how can you expect people to obey you?'

On seeing the engagement ring, the king was flooded with memories and felt very sad. But just then the queen walked in. 'As long as you don't admit to that promise,' she said, smiling coldly, 'who will dare oppose you?' Then, she quickly snatched the ring from Sainaimu's hand and threw it into the fire.

The king and the queen decided the only way to stop their daughter seeing Ailipu was to exile him and his mother. The next day, the king's guards arrived to escort them to the city wall.

Sainaimu knew of her parents' plans and had arranged for Ahe to deliver a message. As Ailipu passed through the city gates, Ahe pressed a note into his hands. Sainaimu's message promised to remain faithful to their love, and in his heart Ailipu swore to return to the city to find her.

Far away in a remote desert town, Ailipu worked as a farmer. The work was hard and exhausting, but Ailipu never complained. Instead, he waited patiently each day to hear word from Sainaimu.

A year later, while selling produce at the town market, he came upon an old beggar from the capital. Ailipu gave the beggar some money and asked him for news from the capital. 'Please tell me if there is any news of the princess Sainaimu,' Ailipu asked.

'I only know that she is ill,' replied the beggar. 'For one year now she has stayed in the palace, and the king and queen are greatly worried for her health. The king has even built a splendid garden for her, but she never leaves her room.'

On hearing this, Ailipu knew that his absence was the cause of Sainaimu's illness. He decided to return to the capital immediately. Saying goodbye to his mother, he set off on his journey across the harsh desert.

When he reached the city, Ailipu sold himself as a slave to the caretakers of the palace. Taking a new name so that he wouldn't be recognised, he convinced the caretakers that he was a poor farmer from the desert. The caretakers assigned Ailipu to take care of the garden, and Ailipu rejoiced at his luck.

Every day Ailipu would pass under Sainaimu's balcony, but she never appeared. He often stood close to the maids as they rested in the garden, hoping to overhear some news about her condition.

One day, a maid walked past Ailipu, carrying roses from the garden for the princess. Ailipu asked the maid to wait, and quickly wrote a note, informing Sainaimu that he was a worker in the gardens. He folded the note inside the bouquet of roses and asked the maid to deliver them to the princess.

When Sainaimu discovered Ailipu's note hidden among the roses, she was overjoyed. She peered out of her balcony, hoping to catch a glimpse of Ailipu, but he was nowhere to be seen.

She quickly dressed and ran to her father's chambers. 'Father,' she said, 'may I visit the garden?'

The king was surprised but happy to see that his daughter was smiling again. 'Of course, my dear,' he said. 'The maids will escort you.'

Sainaimu waited anxiously in the garden, but Ailipu did not arrive. She began to think a cruel joke had been played on her. Just as she was about to leave, she heard a rustling in the bushes.

'Sainaimu,' a voice said, 'I am here, but I cannot come out or we will be discovered. Meet me under the cover of the fruit trees in the orchard.'

Sainaimu ran to the orchard where Ailipu was already waiting for her, his arms outstretched. They happily embraced, and from that day onwards Sainaimu and Ailipu would meet every day in the orchard. Sainaimu's

maids sympathised with their princess and promised not to tell the king or queen of Ailipu's return.

However, there was one maid by the name of Aqi who was jealous of the two lovers. She wanted to separate them, for she had fallen in love with Ailipu herself. One day, when Ailipu was returning to his room, Aqi ran up to him and kissed him on the cheek. 'A slave can never marry a princess,' she said to Ailipu. 'But we are a perfect match!'

Ailipu was furious and pushed Aqi away. 'I will always be devoted to Sainaimu,' he said, walking away, 'even if I am a slave!'

Aqi's face flushed red with anger and embarrassment. She ran straight to the palace to tell the king that Ailipu had returned. The king immediately ordered his soldiers to find Ailipu and throw him in the dungeon. But Sainaimu's maid Ahe had been listening at the door and she ran to warn Ailipu. She quickly hid him in the cellar and then hurried to fetch the princess.

The king's guards searched the entire garden and

palace grounds looking for Ailipu. When they reported back to the king that they could not find him, the king accused Aqi of misleading him. 'Ailipu is not here,' he said. 'You must be lying, and for that I shall have you punished!'

But the queen shook her head. 'Why would she make up such a story if it wasn't true? No, Ailipu must be here. Tell your guards to search inside the palace!'

The king ordered that the search continue and all the exits of the palace be sealed.

But they were too late. Sainaimu had already found Ailipu in the cellar, and together they ran and hid in the orchard. While the guards were reporting to the king, Ahe had arrived and told the two lovers to jump over the garden wall. On the other side, Sainaimu and Ailipu found two horses waiting. They mounted the horses and rode towards the lands in the east where the sun rises. Leaving the king and queen far behind them, they began their new life of freedom and happiness.

Warrior Gunagan and the Sand Devil

A MONGOLIAN TALE

Long ago in Mongolia, there was an extraordinary warrior by the name of Gunagan. Gunagan was famous throughout the prairies of the north for superior strength and his skill on a horse. Because he often used his abilities as a warrior to help and protect others, the people of the north compared him to the majestic eagle that soared high over their lands.

One day, Gunagan had to leave on a hunting expedition far away from his home. As he loaded supplies onto his horse, Gunagan looked at his beautiful wife and felt sorry that he had to leave her alone to take care of the cattle and sheep.

'There is no game to catch in these lands so I must go away,' he said. 'But I will only be gone two or three days at the most.'

Gunagan's wife assured him that she would be fine and helped him to saddle his horse. Then she watched from the entrance of their tent as Gunagan mounted his horse and rode into the distance.

Far away from the prairies, in a dark and distant valley, there lived a sand devil that terrorised herdsmen and their families. The devil was terrifying to look at. He was twice the size of a man, with skin the colour of dark blood. His hands were claw-like, and his mouth had many rows of sharp teeth which he used to eat his prey. Every night, the devil would travel out into the prairies, looking for a lone herdsman or a flock of sheep to feed upon. Sometimes he captured entire families and stole their money and jewels. Then he would imprison the captives in his dungeon and force them to work for him.

The devil knew that Gunagan had a large number of cattle and sheep, and he was jealous that Gunagan had married such a beautiful wife. He longed to rob Gunagan's home and kidnap his wife, but he dared not attempt such a thing for he knew Gunagan was a brave and skilled warrior.

One day, the devil was sitting in his cave when one of his crows flew in and landed at his feet. 'Gunagan goes hunting,' the crow cawed. 'He has left his home.'

The devil's eyes shone with evil. 'Really?' he said. 'Tell me more.'

'His wife is now at home all alone,' the crow continued.

'Ha!' the devil bellowed. 'I must leave at once!'

Standing outside his cave, the devil summoned a sand-storm and travelled under its cover until he arrived at the warrior's tent.

Some herdsmen saw the approach of the sandstorm in the distance and followed it to Gunagan's tent. Sand-storms were always a bad omen on the prairie, so they were on the lookout for possible danger. But the devil was too sneaky; he saw them standing at the entrance of the tent and snuck in through a small flap loosened by the storm.

Gunagan's wife was sleeping near the fire. The devil grabbed her with one arm and snatched one of the burning logs with the other to set fire to the tent. Gunagan's wife struggled against the devil's grip and cried loudly for help, alerting the two guards outside.

They quickly entered the tent with their swords drawn. Realising that he was trapped, the sand devil turned himself into a whirlwind and escaped out the entrance, taking Gunagan's wife with him.

Two days later, Gunagan returned home. As he approached his tent and saw the neighbours gathered outside, he became worried. 'What has happened?' he cried, drawing his horse close to the group.

'The sand devil came two nights ago and has taken your wife!' they answered.

Gunagan was furious. He took up his sword and slung

his bow and arrows across his shoulder. 'I will kill that devil. Where does he live?' he asked.

'We've heard the devil lives in a dark valley where the hills begin,' one of the neighbours said. 'That's also where he keeps many of his captives. Some of them are from our families. You must promise to free them as well.'

Gunagan vowed to return the prisoners and slay the evil devil. Then he rode off towards the hills, leaving a cloud of dust behind.

All through the day and night Gunagan rode like the wind and did not stop until he reached the valley of the sand devil. When he entered, the valley was deadly still and there was nothing but rocks and sand all around him. No breeze stirred and no living animal or plant could be seen.

Gunagan dismounted from his horse and marched across the silent valley. He saw numerous bones scattered on the ground, bleached white from the sun. 'These must be the remains of people who have been devoured by the devil,' he thought. But Gunagan wasn't frightened.

He quickened his pace until he reached the entrance of the sand devil's cave.

Meanwhile, the sand devil had asked Gunagan's wife to marry him, offering her all the treasures in his possession. But she had refused, saying that she would never marry an evil devil like him.

Angered by her answer, the devil had locked her in a cell, giving her three days to change her mind. Now, it was nearly the end of the third day, and the devil was waiting. 'You are so beautiful,' he said. 'I will marry you and you will be queen of my palace.'

Gunagan's wife glared at the devil. 'I will never marry you,' she said, 'and there is nothing you can do to change my mind!'

The devil was enraged and picked up his spear. 'How dare you,' he shouted. 'If you don't obey me, I will kill you!'

Just then, one of the devil's guards ran in. 'Master! Master!' he said. 'Warrior Gunagan is here at the palace!'

The devil quickly let go of Gunagan's wife and ran to the

entrance of the cave. 'Shut the doors!' he yelled, but it was too late. Gunagan had already killed the guard and now stood facing the devil, his sword drawn ready for combat.

With a cry, the devil turned into a whirlwind and flew away. Gunagan ran out of the cave, but he could not find the devil anywhere, for a huge sandstorm had risen up and was blocking his sight.

Just then Gunagan's horse neighed loudly. Gunagan turned and jumped on the horse's back and they galloped up to the mountain top. The devil was sitting on a rock, certain that Gunagan would never find him. When he saw the warrior approach, he jumped up and grabbed his spear.

Gunagan and the devil fought a fierce battle on the mountain peak. Every time the devil tried to stab Gunagan with his spear, the warrior blocked him with his sword. Seeing that he couldn't win the fight, the devil tried to escape by jumping into a lake and swimming to the other side. But Gunagan jumped in after him and they continued fighting in the water.

Finally the devil could stand it no longer and he crawled

out of the lake. He raised his spear above his head and twisted his body, preparing to turn into a whirlwind. But the water had slowed him down. Just as he was ready to fly away, Gunagan plunged his sword into the middle of the whirlwind and knocked the devil to the ground.

Realising that the devil was dead, Gunagan made a fire to burn the body and scattered the ashes over the ground. Then he rode back to the devil's cave and freed his wife. Together, they broke into the other cells and released all the people who had been captured, giving them a share of the devil's treasure. 'I have killed the devil,' Gunagan told them. 'You are free to go!'

After that, Gunagan and his wife returned home. All the neighbours were extremely grateful to Gunagan for defeating the devil and releasing their families. They prepared an extravagant feast with delicious food and wine to welcome him back. From that day onwards, Gunagan became known as a great hero who could rid the land of devils. His praises are still sung today by the herdsmen as they ride across the Mongolian prairies.

The Tale of Ali Mountain

A Gaoshan Tale

A long time ago, in the centre of Taiwan Island, there was a mountain that differed from all the other mountains. No tree, blade of grass, or flower grew there, and no water flowed from its heights to the plains below. Even the wind seemed to stop at the foot of the mountain and turn around, not wanting to climb the steep, barren slopes. Because of its desolate landscape, this mountain was called 'Bald Mountain' by the villagers around it.

In one of these villages, there was a young man

named Ali. He lived a simple life on his own, hunting and gathering food from the forest. Ali had no family, yet because he was strong and brave and always willing to help others, he was a favourite among the villagers and had many friends.

One day, Ali decided to go hunting in the forests that surrounded the foot of Bald Mountain. As he entered the thick woods, he could hear cries for help and rushed towards the sound. Through a small clearing, he saw two young women running towards him. The women screamed in fear, and Ali saw they were being chased by a large tiger.

'Hide behind me!' he shouted, and they dashed behind his back. The tiger growled when he saw Ali in his path and crouched down to pounce on him. But Ali was fast and skilled as a hunter. Using his hunting knife, he stabbed the tiger in its belly, and the great beast tumbled onto its side. Roaring in pain and anger, the tiger finally limped away and disappeared into the thicket.

The two young women were greatly relieved and

thanked Ali for saving them. But just as they did, a strong wind blew through the forest and forced them to cover their heads. Suddenly, an old man with a flowing white beard appeared in the sky above, flying towards them. In his hand he held a sceptre topped with the head of a dragon.

Ali jumped up to defend the two women again, but the old man landed and walked straight past him, ignoring him completely. He grabbed the women roughly by their dresses. 'How dare you?' he shouted. 'Come back with me right now!'

The two women struggled, but did not cry out. Instead, they let the old man drag them towards Bald Mountain.

Ali ran after them. 'Stop!' he shouted at the old man. 'What are you doing? Why are you forcing these women to go with you?'

The old man stopped and turned around to face him. 'It's no concern of yours,' he answered coldly. 'Stay away from us!' Then he pushed the girls forward with his dragon-head sceptre.

Ali didn't think twice; he chased after the old man, grabbed his sceptre and hit him on the head. The old man crumpled to the ground. Ali then shouted to the two women to run away into the forest. When he turned back, he saw the old man pull himself up and fly into the sky. In a matter of seconds, he had disappeared completely into the clouds.

The two women ran back and grabbed Ali's arm. 'Please hurry!' they shouted as they pulled him along, all the while looking towards the sky, which was becoming darker and darker.

By the time they had reached the edge of the forest, the sky was black and lightning flashed menacingly between the heavy clouds. The two women heard the thunder and began to tremble. 'Trouble is coming! Trouble is coming!' they wailed, continuing to pull Ali along.

'But who are you?' he asked. 'Why are you so frightened of the storm?'

But the two women were so terrified they could not answer. Finally, one of the women said, 'We are fairies who have run away from heaven because we want to live on earth. But we have broken the laws of heaven so now the heavens will punish us all!'

'What do you mean?' Ali asked. 'Who is going to be punished?'

The two women looked at each other with tears in their eyes. 'All the people in your village,' they answered. 'The old man you hit is the God of Longevity, and it was his duty to arrest us and take us back to heaven. But you came to our rescue, and now he will report you to the Jade Emperor. The Jade Emperor will have no choice but to ask the God of Thunder to destroy your entire village!'

As they finished speaking, a loud boom of thunder shook the trees around them. 'See? It is happening already!' they said, and began to sob.

Ali was greatly troubled. Although he'd only been trying to help the two fairies, he knew that interfering in the laws of heaven brought disaster.

'Please don't cry,' he pleaded. 'Tell me if there is a way that I can save my village.'

The two fairies looked at him sadly. 'The only way to stop the destruction is to find someone willing to sacrifice himself to the God of Thunder,' they answered.

Suddenly, Ali felt relief and courage flood through his entire body. 'I'm the one who hit the God of Longevity,' he said. 'So I will sacrifice myself to the God of Thunder.'

'No!' the fairies cried out. 'You can't sacrifice yourself! We can't let you pay for the trouble we created.' They pulled Ali along, telling him to flee with them and take cover from the storm.

But Ali stood firm. 'Do not worry,' he said. 'You didn't ask me to fight the God of Longevity, so I am the one who created this trouble, not you. I cannot let the people of my village suffer because of me. I must go. There is no other way.' With these words, Ali broke free from their grip and ran back towards the mountain.

'I am coming, God of Thunder!' he shouted in a great booming voice. As he neared the top of the mountain, the black clouds swirled towards him and away from the village below. Ali held up the dragon-head sceptre and pointed it at the sky. 'God of Thunder, I am the one who saved the fairies and hit the God of Longevity,' he cried. 'Throw your thunderbolts at me!'

Immediately, the God of Thunder sent a huge bolt of lightning towards Ali. The light around Ali grew brighter, and began to crackle and spark. Yet Ali was not harmed. Then the God of Thunder sent a flurry of lightning at Ali, until he was covered in a ball of white light. He began to glow like a blazing sun, and the two fairies covered their eyes from the searing light, unable to look at him any more.

Suddenly, the sky went quiet. The two fairies glanced up and saw that the storm had vanished. They looked over to where Ali had been standing, but instead saw that the mountain was now covered in cypress trees and green grass. One of the trees was a strange, unique shape and pointed straight up towards the clouds. The two fairies realised it was the dragon-head sceptre.

People from the village began to arrive. They had heard the loud storm and come to investigate. Everyone

rejoiced that Bald Mountain was no longer bald, but covered in lush forest.

'Ali died to save us all,' the two fairies explained, 'and now he has become the trees and grass on the mountain. We want to stay in the human world, so we will become the flowers to keep him company.' As soon as the fairies finished speaking they disappeared, and suddenly the mountain was dotted with beautiful, delicate flowers.

In memory of Ali and his sacrifice, the people of the village renamed the mountain 'Ali Mountain'. To this day, it remains one of the most beautiful mountains in Taiwan, and people still visit to wander among its abundant forests and flowers.

The Legend of Lady White Snake

Long, long ago, near the West Lake of Hangzhou, there lived a white snake who dreamed of becoming immortal. The snake was very gentle and kind, and performed many good deeds every day. On the banks of the same lake was a turtle who also wanted to become immortal. But this turtle was greedy and rude, and always looked for short-cuts.

One day the white snake and the turtle fought, but the turtle was no match for the snake's powers and he ran away, defeated, towards the hills in the west.

Meanwhile, after a thousand years of study and training, the white snake was finally able to visit the human world. She took on the form of a beautiful woman, and so did her sister, who was a green snake. The white snake took the name of Bai Suzhen and wore a white dress, while her younger sister took the name of Xiao Qing and wore a green dress.

The two sisters decided to visit the human world on the festival of Spring Remembrance. Standing on the shore of the West Lake, the two women delighted in the scenes of holiday celebration around them. Suddenly, though, it began to rain, and the two sisters hurried under a large tree for cover. The rain became a heavy downpour, and the sisters, barely sheltered by the tree, were beginning to regret their decision to visit the West Lake.

Soon, a young man with an umbrella came walking along the path. Seeing the two sisters huddled under the tree, he offered them protection from the rain. The two sisters readily agreed and all three stood under the umbrella, waiting for the rain to stop.

The young man's name was Xu Xian, and Bai Suzhen could not help from peeping at his handsome face. Xiao Qing saw her sister looking and smiled. When the rain began to subside, she suggested that they travel home together by boat. As the boatman rowed to the other side of the lake, he sang a song:

To ride in the same boat,
you must do good deeds for ten lives;
To be together as husband and wife,
you must do good deeds for one hundred lives.

On hearing this, Bai Suzhen and Xu Xian looked at each other and blushed. When they reached the dock, Xu Xian insisted that Bai Suzhen keep the umbrella, in case it started to rain again on their journey home. Bai Suzhen was about to decline when Xiao Qing suddenly accepted for her, telling Xu Xian they would visit him the following day to return his umbrella.

When the two sisters arrived at Xu Xian's house the

next morning, he told them he was a poor man with no family, and that he worked at a pharmacy to earn his living. Bai Suzhen did not care that he was poor; she admired his kindness and honesty. As she and Xu Xian talked, they fell in love.

As the months passed, Bai Suzhen and Xu Xian decided to get married. They had a small but happy wedding and moved to the city of Zhenjiang. Together, the newly wed couple opened their own pharmacy. Because of Bai Suzhen's powers, she was a magnificent doctor, able to cure patients no matter what illness they had. Before long the store became famous and the customers nicknamed Bai Suzhen 'Lady White', for she always wore a white dress.

One year, a terrible sickness called the plague swept through the province. People began dying, and soon the plague had spread to the city of Zhenjiang. When Lady White heard what was happening, she asked her husband to prepare a special medicine. Then she told him to hang a sign on the pharmacy door that said: 'No charge for the poor and the sick'.

Because the medicine was magic, everyone who took Lady White's formula soon recovered. They sang the praises of Lady White and her kind husband, Xu Xian.

It wasn't long before news of Lady White reached the leader of the Jinshan Temple, a monk called Fa Hai. But Fa Hai was no ordinary monk; he was the turtle who'd fought Lady White when she was still a snake. After he lost the battle, he hid in a Buddhist temple for a thousand years and waited to regain his strength. During that time, he stole three magic tools which used to belong to Buddha: a golden bowl, a robe and a blue dragon sceptre. Using the robe, he took on the human form of a monk. Then he used the power of the blue dragon sceptre to kill the head monk of Jinshan Temple and take his position.

When he heard that Lady White had become famous, Fa Hai was furious. He knew Lady White was really the white snake that had defeated him all those years ago.

Fa Hai thought day and night about how he could get his revenge. Finally, he came up with a devious plan. He followed Lady White's husband in the street one day and told him, 'My son, I see that you have a black light hovering above your head. Such a light only surrounds those who keep company with devils.'

Xu Xian was shocked. 'You must be mistaken,' he said.

But Fa Hai shook his head. 'I'm afraid not. I have heard rumours that your wife is a white snake disguised as a woman.'

Xu Xian's face flushed red with anger. 'How dare you say such a thing!' he said. 'My wife is a noble lady.'

'If you don't believe me,' continued Fa Hai, 'then get her to drink some wine at the Dragon Boat Festival. If she drinks the wine, then she will have to return to her original form.'

Xu Xian was greatly troubled by the monk's words, and wished to prove him wrong. On the night of the Dragon Boat Festival, he took a glass of wine to his wife. 'Come,' he said. 'It is tradition to drink wine tonight to drive away evil spirits. Let us drink together.'

But Lady White shook her head. 'I am pregnant and cannot drink.'

Xu Xian felt a stab of worry. 'Just a little,' he pressed. 'You have been working for days, and tonight is a celebration. A little won't do you any harm.'

Lady White finally agreed and drank the glass of wine her husband gave her. After a little while, she began to feel faint. She knew something was wrong and told Xu Xian she was going to rest in the bedroom.

It wasn't long before Xu Xian began to worry about his wife and went to check up on her. When he lifted the canopy on the bed frame, he saw a huge white snake in the bed. He cried out in fright and then fainted.

When Lady White had recovered enough to return to her human form, she saw her husband lying unconscious on the floor. He'd had such a fright, he was close to death. Lady White asked her sister to watch over him, then used her powers to fly to Kunlun Mountain to find a magic plant.

When she returned home, she mixed up the correct medicine and placed a few drops on Xu Xian's frozen lips. Soon, colour spread over his face and he sat up,

looking in shock at Lady White. 'You tricked me!' he said.

'I have just saved your life because of my love for you. How can you say I tricked you?' she answered.

But Xu Xian was still convinced that Lady White meant him harm, and he jumped out of bed and ran straight to Jinshan Temple.

When Fa Hai heard Xu Xian's cries outside the temple door, he knew that his plan had succeeded. He let Xu Xian in and told him not to leave, knowing that Lady White would soon arrive to find her husband.

Lady White and her sister followed Xu Xian to the temple and watched as the monk ushered him in. They realised Fa Hai was the turtle from long ago, and that he must have told Xu Xian that Lady White was a snake. Standing outside the temple gates, they demanded to see Xu Xian, but Fa Hai would not let them in. He grabbed his blue dragon sceptre and pointed it towards the nearby river to create a giant storm. Waves began to crash against the banks and spill over onto the land.

Soon Lady White and her sister were waist-deep in water. Fearing that they would drown, Lady White took out a golden hairpin from her hair and transformed it into a boat. Then she and her sister climbed in and looked for a way to get inside the temple walls.

Xu Xian realised that his wife had come to rescue him and felt bad for doubting her. Climbing the temple walls, he called out, 'Over here!'

Lady White saw him waving and steered the boat in his direction. Xu Xian quickly jumped in and they fled back home to the other side of the river.

'I heard you fighting with Fa Hai,' Xu Xian explained. 'And I know now that you would never harm me. I love you no matter what your form.'

Lady White was overjoyed to hear her husband's words, and the two vowed to stay together forever.

Before long, Xu Xian and Lady White's son was born. Thirty days after the birth, the whole family came together at their house to celebrate the birth. Fa Hai heard about the celebration and realised it was another chance to get revenge on Lady White. Disguising himself in normal clothes, he snuck in with a crowd of well-wishers. He waited until Lady White was sitting alone in her room, then crept up behind her and held his magic golden bowl over her head. Instantly, Lady White turned back into a snake. Fa Hai captured her under his bowl and darted out of the house. To make sure that Lady White would be trapped forever, Fa Hai buried the golden bowl under a pagoda beside the West Lake.

When Xu Xian discovered that Lady White was missing, he knew that something terrible had happened and went straight to Jinshan Temple. But he was too late, for Fa Hai had disappeared and no one knew where he was.

Xu Xian searched everywhere for Lady White but could not find her. He asked Xiao Qing for help, but she did not have enough power to fight Fa Hai. Finally, Xu Xian gave up and went home, full of sadness.

Then one day, after many years away, Xiao Qing returned to the human world. She had acquired many magical powers and now knew that Fa Hai had imprisoned Lady White under the West Lake pagoda. Using her powers, she created a great thunderstorm over the West Lake. Thunder boomed and a huge bolt of lightning struck the pagoda, causing it to collapse. Lady White walked out from the rubble and together the two sisters set off to find Xu Xian.

When Xu Xian saw his wife, he was ecstatic, for in his heart he had never stopped believing that one day they would be reunited. Lady White, Xu Xian and their son spent the rest of their lives living happily together.

As for Fa Hai, he lost his magical tools because of his evil ways. So when Xiao Qing and Lady White went to find him, he was powerless to fight them and ran away to hide in the belly of a crab. Once he was there, he realised with horror that he was too weak to escape and would be trapped forever. And that is why the inside of a crab is orange, the same colour as a monk's robe.